Tales by the World's
Great Contemporary Writers
Presented Unabridged

All selections in
Short Story International
are published full and
unabridged.

Editor
Sylvia Tankel

Associate Editor
Erik Sandberg-Diment

Contributing Editor
John Harr

Assistant Editors
Mildred Butterworth
Debbie Kaufman
Kirsten Hammerle

Art Director
Carol Anderson

Circulation Director
Nat Raboy

Production Director
Michael Jeffries

Business Manager
John O'Connor

Publisher
Sam Tankel

Volume 15, Number 88, October 1991.
Short Story International (USPS 375-970)
Copyright © by International Cultural
Exchange 1991. Printed in U.S.A. All rights
reserved. Reproduction in whole or in part
prohibited. Second class postage paid at
Great Neck, N.Y. 11022 and at additional
mailing offices. **Editorial offices: P.O. Box
405, Great Neck, N.Y. 11022.** Enclose
stamped, self-addressed envelope with
submission. One year (six issues) subscription
for U.S., U.S. possessions $24, Canada $27
(US), other countries $29 (US). Single copy
price $5.45 (US). **For subscriptions and
address changes write to *Short Story
International*, P.O. Box 405, Great
Neck, N.Y. 11022.** *Short Story
International* is published bimonthly by
International Cultural Exchange, 6 Sheffield
Road, Great Neck, N.Y. 11021. Postmaster
please send Form 3579 to P.O. Box 405,
Great Neck, N.Y. 11022.

Note from the Editor

Long before written language, story tellers would mesmerize both the young and old.

In this issue, A.E. Sturges of Australia takes us "fossicking" when the economy goes sour. It means leaving family and modern comforts. When his protagonist finds his golden nugget, he is faced with a decision: which way of life to pursue.

A way of life is also finally chosen by Gerhart Drucker's caring American protagonist. His startling surprise is his complaining wife's reaction to his action.

Some persons come to regret their choices. Ke Zhaojin's Red Plum, attractive and self-sufficient, rejects several forthright suitors, thinking they will not do her justice when married. The man who keeps her guessing, who tells very little about himself, excites her. In time, married to him, he takes her from China to the USA where he still keeps her uninformed of his doings, but now she finds herself a cowering lost soul.

Another change of country is significant in Jerome Mandel's "The Orange." Coming from Chicago to Tel Aviv, his undaunted, successful protagonist learns from personal experience the concern hoodlums cause anywhere in the world.

Each story in this issue has its humor, drama, and "lesson," as in the oral stories in days of yore, that engross the reader and leave him thinking...questioning.

Copyrights and acknowledgments

We wish to express deep thanks to the authors, translators, publishers and literary agents for their permission to publish the stories in this issue.

"The Discovery" by A.E. Sturges originally appeared in *Westerly*. Copyright A.E. Struges. "The Lost of Paradise" by Colin Leslie Beadon. Copyright © 1991 Colin Leslie Beadon. "Red Plum" by Ke Zhaojin, 1991. "Wednesday Morning: a Christmas Conspiracy Tale" from *My Merry Mornings: Stories from Prague* by Ivan Klíma. Translation by George Theiner. Published by Readers International, Inc. English translation copyright ©1985 Readers International, Inc. "The Six Thousandth Bird" by Nigel Watt, 1991. "The Orange" by Jerome Mandel, 1991. "Tanabata's Wife" by Sinai C. Hamada originally appeared in *Graphic*. Copyright Sinai C. Hamada. "The Masterpiece" from *Nuestro milenio* by Paloma Díaz-Mas. Published by Editorial Anagrama, 1987. Translation by Phyllis Zatlin, 1991. "The Deck Chair" by Ali Elmak originally appeared in *Sudanou*. Copyright Ali Elmak. Translation by Hume Alexander Horan. "Goat Water" by Barbara Gilson. Copyright 1991 Barbara Gilson. "The Sacred Number Seven" by Gerhart A. Drucker, 1991. "The Present Day" by Sergei Yesin appeared in *Soviet Literature*, 1989. Translation by Andrew Bromfield. By permission. "The Inferno" by Fadil Hadzich. Copyright Fadil Hadzich. English translation by Josip Novakovich. 1991.

Photo credit: Ivan Klímo © Ivan Kyncl.

Table of Contents

"That was what was wrong with this life: he had no home."

The Discovery

BY A.E. STURGES

MULLIGAN looked at the sun. Pushing five, still stinking hot. Make this the last. He swirled the pan deftly, watched the light stuff spill over the lip. Despite his tiredness he felt the familiar thrill with each pan, more intense with the last of the day. The same question formed: would this be the one to show promise of more than grub stakes? He laughed at himself bitterly. Always it was the next pan, the next day, the next week, the next, the next. Couldn't give up, might miss by one. Fever. More dog-in-the-manger than fever, frightened of missing out, of leaving it for the next bloke. He shook the heavy stuff from the groove, picked it over, put in the bottle the few pieces that showed color. He rose, stretched his aching back, picked up his coat and billy.

"Come on!"

The spaniel bounded forward, quivering, eager for the rough caress. He too stretched, then trotted after Mulligan along the track they'd worn from hut to creek.

"Wonder what's our luck."

The dog closed up, right on Mulligan's heels as he left the track and pushed through a curtain of scrub into a rough clearing. From here a network of narrow pads ran down through the scrub to the creek. Across one a rabbit lay, still warm.

"Bloody bunny! Ain't there no wallaby left?"

The dog looked askance at Mulligan's tone. He frisked about, urging Mulligan to hurry, tasting the rabbit, hearing the crunch of the bones. Mulligan freed the mangled leg, reset the trap, broke a bough and brushed the earth, picked up billy, coat and rabbit.

"Bunny bloody stew."

The dog ignored him, indifferent to the vegetables Mulligan had grown against odds, fighting the bracken fern, netting out rabbits and wallaby, wombat and bandicoot, covering against birds the young plants and seeds, cursing the quartz as he dug drains from the creek, cursing the size of roo dung as he gathered it for fertilizer. Determined not to rot in the fossickers' rut of damper, bacon and tea, he had stuck at it grimly, succeeding at last in raising potatoes and carrots, pumpkins and parsnips, onions and silver beet, concentrating on crops he could store, or that, like the beet, replenished itself as he broke it leaf by leaf. The sun was low when they reached the hut, but its light lay warm and gold on the pool Mulligan had scooped from the creek where it turned behind the hut. Mulligan lit the fire, left ready set as always, skinned and washed the rabbit, tossed some to the dog. Put the rest in the stew billy with water and salt, added potato, carrot and onion, and hung it on the fire.

Then he stripped naked, draping his work clothes on a box before the fire, took soap and towel and trotted to the pool, grumbling at the sinking sun, as he went.

"Burns you to a cinder when you've got to work, then hides behind the hill when you want a bloody bath."

He stood on the moss at the edge of the pool, sluicing and soaping in readiness for his bath. A kookaburra laughed harshly nearby, and Mulligan scowled up, touchy in his nakedness.

"Laugh, you bastard, laugh."

He gammoned to aim a gun, then plunged into the pool,

splashing and blowing until his bones began to numb. He sprang out, rubbed himself vigorously, then ran to the hut, the fire burning his skin as he pulled on his spare set of clothes.

He shook the stew billy, got plate and knife and fork. Mixed flour in a tin with water and salt, kneading the dough to a small flat loaf. The fire had burned down to a mound of glowing coals. Mulligan scooped a hole, dropped in the dough, covered it with coals. Put on the tea billy, got mug and sugar and tea. When the water boiled he prised off the lid and threw in the tea, lifted off the billy and tapped it with a stick. Raised the lid of the stew billy and prodded with his fork. The savory smell of stew filled the hut. Mulligan tipped it on his plate and drew up his box to the fire.

The spaniel crept in and sat quiet, watching Mulligan eat. Mulligan ate on, pretending not to see him. At last the dog, anxious at the speed with which the stew was disappearing, growled softly, then louder.

"What's the matter with you? Had yours, didn't you? And I thought you didn't like stew."

The dog's eyes dumbly appealed.

"Bloody glutton! Here!"

Mulligan tossed meat through the doorway. The dog streaked after it. Mulligan swallowed the rest of his stew, poured a mug of tea, and while it cooled, scraped the coals from the damper. He looked at it critically, then lifted it out and set it to cool on the hearth.

Tea over, Mulligan felt the nightly craving for a smoke. To combat it, he turned his thoughts to home. Home. That was what was wrong with this life: he had no home. A dog in place of family. The change had been forced on him—mill closed, jobs non-existent. He'd sworn never to accept the dole. Work or starve, that was his motto. So he'd gone fossicking.

Fossicking had drawn him since the time he'd spent his holidays scratching for osmiridium at Black Creek. It had been a hard row, but he'd slaved to make it pay, enough to keep the home going, educate the kids. Yes, he'd battled it through. But a man missed his family. One day he'd strike it rich, make a packet, then head for home. Till then, he must make do with memory.

Milly: what would Milly be doing? Queer to think that day by day as he went to the creek and panned the gravel and sand, other people in other places were going about their business, each wrapped in his own thoughts, his own ambitions, troubles, pleasure, pain...Milly would probably be by the wireless, a pile of darning beside her, high as the seat of her chair. Wherever Milly was, there was mending; it was a family joke. A good wife, Milly, hard-working, steady, never one to gad about, putting the kids first, starving herself in the hard days so that they had enough. Good-looker, too—or had been. It was now so long since he'd seen her that he couldn't call her face to mind. It was there, tantalizing, just beyond his vision. He could feel it, see details, the tilt of the nose, the set of the eyes, but the whole face refused to come into focus.

He shook his head, turned his thoughts to Beryl. Dancing, no doubt. Always a lively one, Beryl! Or at the pictures with a beau. Always plenty of boys when Beryl was about. Good-looking kid, and smart as they come. Kid? *Struth!* She'd be, no, yes, twenty-seven this June! God, how the years slipped by. Wonder she wasn't married. Perhaps she was. But no, they'd have let him know, somehow.

Then Rod—Rod must be twenty-three. A man. Need no help now to assemble his bike. He'd have a car. But they'd had some fun on the old bikes, off early on a Sunday, lunch in their knapsacks, more like two cobbers than father and son. Fishing the lake and river, shooting for rabbit and roo, picking watercress or mushrooms to take home for tea. And further back still, when Rod was a little boy, the kites he'd made for him, cross, bowie and boxie, and they'd held them together on top of Sky Hill against the tug of the westerly wind, sending up messages, watching them buck and dive.

Yes, that's what was missing. Family outings, evenings round the fire. The sharing of pleasure and sorrow. The sense of family.

A coal fell from the fire. Mulligan jerked awake, poked the coals together. Lit a candle, and read for a time from the Bible, the only book he had, and from which he drew unlimited satisfaction, not knowing or wondering why.

Before he went to bed, Mulligan stood for awhile in the doorway of the hut, looking out at the hills, listening to noises of the night: the cry of a mopoke, the creaking of trees, the thump of a wallaby's tail, the soughing of leaves in the wind.

Mulligan woke, refreshed, from a nine-hour sleep. He put a match to the fire, pulled on his clothes, and *sluiced* his hands and face. The sun was already warm, the air still with the promise of heat. High in a tree by the creek a magpie sang to the sun.

Mulligan cooked some oats, ate them with a spoonful of his precious condensed milk. The dog watched him.

"All right, all right, don't get impatient. There'll be bunny for you down the track."

Over the coals Mulligan grilled two rashers of bacon, carefully catching the fat to spread on the damper for lunch. He washed up, put out the fire, reset it, put his lunch in the billy.

"Come on!"

The dog ran ahead, eager for the promised rabbit. Mulligan walked evenly, refusing to be hurried, the sun warm on his bare head, the billy swinging from his hand.

The dog barked excitedly. Mulligan looked up. A long fawn shape streaked up the bank, followed close by the dog. A hare! Make a nice change for the pot. Laughing at himself for a fool, Mulligan ran through the bracken, up the bank after the dog.

At the top he stopped, panting for breath. Of hare or dog there was no sign. He turned. Behind lay the doll's-house hut, below him and closer the winding creek showed silver between the wattles. Mulligan felt a sudden impulse to toss a stone in the creek. He stopped and put out his hand as the spaniel broke from the fern.

"What?"

The dog stared at Mulligan as Mulligan stooped, stared at the stone, as if he too were stone. "A nugget," Mulligan whispered, "a bloody great nugget, a nugget the size of my fist. I'm seeing things, gone mad, shouldn't stoop at my age, or rush up a bank like a bull." He straightened, looked away, tearing his gaze from the ground. Then suddenly looked again. Still there. Damn near solid gold. Was he dreaming? Make sure. He swung to the dog.

"Boxer!"

The dog crouched low, worried at Mulligan's mood. Mulligan walked a few unsteady steps, then whipped back wildly, scared of losing the spot.

"Real!"

He dropped to his knees, picked up the nugget, weighing, assessing, whispering to himself.

"Must be worth—"

He got to his feet, the nugget heavy in his hand, and stared unseeing out over the creek.

He could go back. No need now to scratch and pan. Go back to comfort, his family, the city.

Instead of the expected elation, Mulligan felt flat. His mind ran now on what he would leave: the hut, the fire, the savory stew. The pool, cold, clear, that washed away fatigue. The garden, won with sweat, choked again with fern; the birds, trees, space, the blessed silence. The dog.

He looked at the dog. The dog looked back, thumped the earth with his tail, whined. Good company, faithful, quiet. Milly, for all her good points, could not keep quiet for a second; her tongue went on and on about everything, about nothing. And Beryl and Rod, what a pair to bicker, snapping and snarling whenever they met; and never satisfied, wanting this, wishing that.

"You want to go back?"

The dog barked sharply once.

"Why? Don't you want company? A mate? Think, now, think! What's there here for you in the end but loneliness and old age? I reckon we better go back."

The dog growled disagreement.

"All right, then, we won't. But if we stay, what do we do with this? Can't run into town and cash it, and then come back. There'd be hundreds pouring out here, and bang'd go our peace. We could hide it in the hut, I suppose, and cash it when we wish. No, you're right, it'd spoil it all, we'd know it was there, be thinking of it all the time, know that we needn't work, a couple of fakes."

He stood distracted, the nugget in his hand. A kookaburra

lighted above his head, and laughed its scorn at the madman and his dog.

"You again! I'll make you laugh!"

Mulligan hurled the nugget, the bird flapped and squawked in alarm the nugget fell full in the creek. Feeling it gone, Mulligan felt wonderfully free, he threw up his arms, shouted loud in relief.

"Gone and a bloody good riddance!"

A thought struck him. He turned to the dog.

"What say we celebrate? We haven't had a holiday since I don't know when. How about we go round the Hump after roo?"

The dog yelped its joy, raced madly round and round, galloped away, turning to coax Mulligan on.

"All right, all right. Don't go stupid. No sense in rushing off. We have to go back to the hut. Got to get the gun, haven't we?"

Born in 1916, in Sydney, A.E. Sturges is presently a university lecturer. He worked in industry for 15 years before starting a working tour of Australia with his wife; they did grape-picking, grain harvesting, hospital domestic work and engineering drafting. About 100 of his short stories, and some verse, have been published in periodicals and literary magazines. His work is included in anthologies in Australia, UK, USA and USSR. His story "Ten-Stitch Tyro" appeared in SSI No. 81.

"There is nothing wrong with you or your face."

The Lost of Paradise

BY COLIN LESLIE BEADON

I did not know Cole Robinson all that well. He was one of those people you run into on a small island, and I had run into him over a number of years. He was a lonely sort, I never ran into him with anybody. He seemed perpetually aloof and withdrawn. I suppose it was this that interested me so much in him.

"How is the writing going?" I asked him one evening. We were sitting in the Ship Inn. I had come in from a long sail from St. Vincent. There had not been much wind and it had taken me a day and a night, and much of another day. It had raised my thirst too. I had come into the noisy, crowded establishment and found him sitting alone down one end of the bar, as though the place was quite empty. He had the ability to do such things.

"I wrote one good paragraph today," he said soberly. "It has not been easy lately. I'm stale, I guess. I don't know what's wrong with me, Brommage."

"Probably nothing more than a drink or two won't fix," I said.

"I've been hoping it was something like that for the last month. Unfortunately, I've found no consolation in the stuff, I don't know what it is. I don't know."

"You're not sick or anything are you?" I asked, looking at him closely. He seemed as sunburnt and well as I'd ever seen him.

"No. Nothing like that. I keep my usual routine. Swim in the early morning, long walk in the evening."

"Maybe you should change that around," I said, ordering two more of the draft beer they had just begun importing from St. Vincent.

He turned on me in horror.

"Oh, I couldn't do that, Brommage. It's out of the question." His fingers slid nervously to his pack of cigarettes.

"Maybe it's your love life," I said, keeping my eye on him from the corner of my face. I was interested to see his reaction, having never seen him with a woman, or anybody else for that matter.

"Really, Brommage. Really. Will you look at me? Now what woman in her right mind would go anywhere with a face like this."

He was very serious about it. I looked at him. He wasn't beautiful, of course. There was vitality in the great brown eyes. He was rugged though, like a rhino is rugged. His large brow was crossed with deep lines, and although he was quite a young man, about thirty or so, there were crows feet in the corners of his eyes, and maybe just the hint of sadness in the eyes.

"Cole," I said to him, "I've one or two friends in Trinidad, very ugly indeed. They have the most beautiful wives. There is nothing wrong with you or your face."

He apeared to consider this for some moments. He was quite a successful writer; he had not hit the best seller list yet, but somehow I felt he might, one day. He seemed to have the inner determination needed. After all, in a few respects, I knew somebody very much like him. Except that she was a painter, and very beautiful.

"I don't know, Brommage," he said. "I don't seem to get anywhere with women. I never have. When I was young, the first girl I ever met, ran away screaming in fright."

I looked at all the beautiful women there that night. Some were local, some from other islands, and some, of course were tourists. The Christmas months are a great mingling time on our island.

"I don't think any one of these women would run away from you screaming," I said.

"I don't know, Brommage. I don't know. I don't know what to say to them to begin with. Here we live in the middle of paradise, and I don't know what to talk about."

"You should let them do all the talking. Just listen intently, and nod your head," I told him.

"Oh I don't know, Brommage." He squirmed in his seat, seemed as though he would say something, and then changed his mind. He kept his hands together, like a closed book, with just the cigarette between his fingers, its smoke meandering like the smoke from a wood fire on a hot windless summer's day. His eyes looked away into space, and he seemed quite contented, though oblivious to the gay throb around us. And then when I thought he had lapsed into a permanent silence, he pulled his great hulk together.

"But what about you, Brommage? Are you leading me to believe everything in your life is just as you wish it?"

"It should be, but it's not," I told him. "My yacht is impounded in St. Vincent, problems with the captain. It's a long, long story and I would not wish to bore you with it."

"Oh yes," he said, sitting up as though he had smelled something. "It sounds quite interesting. Maybe there is something I could use in it. You never know in these things."

"It would take a novel to tell you all the horrors I've been through with my yacht," I told him.

"Really," he said. His eyebrows lifted and the lines on his forhead deepened further, like a furrowed field. "I thought you told me you had sailed back from St Vincent."

"I did. But not on Draconis. I came back with another yacht."

I spent two hours giving him the details of what had happened. He absorbed everything like a huge hungry sponge, stopping me on this point or that. I really think he believed he could use it. It was interesting, I suppose. I just wished it was not happening to me.

At the end, he said, "What an intrigue. You must admit it does have potential. You must be worried over it."

"Worried is an understatement," I said bitterly. "You don't know what happens to a yacht when it's impounded."

"I don't," he said. "What does happen?"

"You lose half your gear and the yacht goes to hell."

"It is difficult to believe people can do such things to each other," he said, "but I know they do. If they didn't, there would not be so much to write about. Greed is the essence of many novels."

"What about love? I thought love was the number one," I said, trying to forget my worries. I raised my glass, "To greed and love."

"To love and greed," he said. "You have to keep the perspective right."

"Ah love," I said. "Now that is far more interesting."

"Yes, well, love," he hesitated. "There's this girl, woman really, I see on the beach sometimes. Just see her, you understand. I've tried to talk to her," he hesitated again. "Well, I don't know, Brommage. It's just a foolish thing." He lapsed into silence, folding his hands once more like a closed book.

"Tell me about her," I said. "I've told you my problems."

He squirmed in his seat, changed the subject, and though I turned him back, he was quite closed about it, for now.

I walked home along the noisy streets. There were many cars and people about. The moon shone in the trees, on the beach to my left, the streets, and in the faces of the people who passed me by.

When I got home, the light was on in my sister's room. She lived and worked in the top of our house. Our house stood way back in sugar-cane fields. There was a long line of casurinas on each side of the drive and behind the house. It was a great plantation house of bulky white coral block; it glowed beautifully in the moonlight and threw deep dark shadows into the base of the trees and wherever the moon did not reach. There were fireflies in the night and a light breeze from the east.

Not wanting to think of my own problem, I thought of my acquaintance Cole Robinson. There was sombody else I knew like him. But she was my beautiful sister, Lydia.

How often had Lydia and I run this same drive in the early morning, down the bumpy marl drive strewn with fallen casurina needles and tiny cones uncomfortable to our feet, across the road and onto the beach, to plunge heedless into the early frothing sea? I did not go to the beach much with her now, having to get to work early. But Lydia always went, even in the rain. I doubt she ever missed a day. I could still remember her as a kid: long raven black hair streaming out behind her as she raced me through the waves for the barrier of the reef.

At that point, something struck me and I stopped, looked up at the light in her window, and then putting the thought away, I shook my head.

I let myself into the dark house, drank some icewater from the fridge in the kitchen and then climbed the stairs. I did not go into my room but went on up the other stairway to the top floor. I stood and listened outside Lydia's room. The moon filled the landing from the open window and the lace curtain billowed in the light breeze.

"Come in, Brommage," came her soft voice. I opened the door softly and swung it back, blinking from the bright lamps she worked under.

Lydia was on the floor where she always worked. She raised her dark violet eyes to me and smiled. Around her on the floor were sheets of unfinished work, paints and brushes in profusion. Her easel stood unused in a corner. She hardly ever used it. It was a lovely room hung with much of her work. Her bed was light blue and neat and there were bright yellow Alamanda flowers in a bowl on her dressing table. They were her favorite flowers, I think.

"My own special brother," she said, pulling herself off the floor. She waltzed up to me and flung her arms around my neck and kissed me. "You smell of beer," she said. "You could at least have brought one home for me."

"I thought you would have been asleep," I said. "Anyhow I would have probably consumed it before I got home."

"Let's make some coffee," she said. She had a small fridge and single element stove in her room. Lydia was organized to a degree. She slid away from me and went about her preparations. She liked strong dark coffee, heaped with spoonfulls of brown Barbados sugar.

I looked at her work. I always looked at it. There were seascapes and views, estate homes and small drooping villages. There was a cat in the sun. She had won a scholarship for her water paints, and it was all she ever used. She had become quite well known on the islands and her fame was spreading rapidly. I watched her at the stove. Her hair fell down like ravensilk, forming over the trim contours of her nymph-like body.

"Lydia," I began. "Have you ever heard of Cole Robinson?" She turned her small perfect little girl's face to watch me.

"Cole Robinson? Cole Robinson?" her face deepened to a woman's frown. "Isn't he a writer?" she said. "Why do you ask?"

"I just wondered," I said. "Have you ever seen him?"

"Nope. I don't know what he looks like. Why?"

"I just wondered," I said.

She gave me a funny look.

"Brommage. Brommage. I hope you are not up to mischief. I hope you are not...not..."

"Matchmaking again," I said quickly, laughing.

"By the way," she turned her dark eyes on me, her head swiveling over her shoulder, "there is somebody I would like you to meet."

"Lydia. Really," I admonished.

"No, honestly. She would be good for you. You worry me sometimes, Brommage. Ever since Lisa, you've closed the shop."

"Ever since Lisa," I said, and left it at that.

My own problems and work kept me fully absorbed for a month or so. And then I ran into Cole Robinson again. It was at the Carib this time. As usual, he sat at the end of the bar, musing by himself. It was quite late and his eyes were a little puffed. We sat talking and enjoying the night breeze. He was not making a great deal of sense, but it didn't matter.

"I'm terribly stuck on one thing or another," he said. "Can't get it going somehow. Not even a good sentence. 'Course I been through it before. It's called writer's block or something stupid. The dark night of the soul."

"You'll get out of it," I said. "You probably need a holiday. Get away somewhere. Come sailing. That'll clear your mind."

"Do you think it would, Brommage? Do you really think so?" He turned his great brown infinitely serious eyes on me.

"It would. Guaranteed to clear away all webs, broken hearts, tabanca."

"Tabanca? What's tabanca?" he asked suspiciously.

"The pain from a horning," I said laughing. "It's a Trinidad expression."

"Oh I'm glad. That's one thing I don't have. I must remember that. Tabanca, you say."

We drank quite a bit that night. I drank in celebration. It was good to have my yacht back again. It had cost me some good money in lawyers' fees and so forth. Yachts always do get you into binds like that. It is the occupational hazard of loving and owning them. I don't know why Cole Robinson was drinking so much. He did not usually go that far, saying that it destroyed him the next day and left him unable to do anything of value.

"You know, Brommage," he said after one of his long brooding silences, "there's this girl I see on the beach. Have I told you before?"

"You never mentioned it," I said lying.

"Well there's this girl. I see her every morning when I go down to take my swim. She's a woman you know. But she seems more like a girl."

"Uh ha," I said. "Most girls become women when they get older."

"You don't understand, Brommage. She's a woman all right, but she seems more like a girl. It's not the way she behaves or anything. I can't put my finger on it."

"Have you ever spoken to her," I asked.

"What? Oh yes. I spoke to her once or twice. I gathered up my courage and spoke to her. She's difficult to speak to, you know. She's unapproachable."

"I suppose many women are, on a beach at that early hour, before they have had coffee."

"Do you really think that is it, Brommage?"

"It could be. Why don't you take down a flask with you and offer her some when you both get out of the sea."

"What a splended idea, Brommage. Do you think it would work?"

"It's gallant. I don't know if it would work. No sugar in the coffee. Remember that, won't you? It's bad for the figure."

"No sugar you say. I must remember that. I don't like it without heaps of brown sugar myself."

That night I did stagger back with two bottles of beer for Lydia, but she was asleep. I sat on a big deep-cushoned chair, on the veranda off my bedroom, drank the two bottles of beer and savored the night. There was no moon, but the sky hung brilliant with stars. Sometime about dawn I woke, still in the chair. I was stiff with the cold of the night and I got up and stretched. Slowly my mind came into gear and I went down to the kitchen. Putting the kettle to boil, I heard Lydia tripping down from upstairs; the front door opened, and then closed behind her. From the kitchen window I saw her small elfin form running for the beach in her old toweling shirt. It came to me then, in a brilliant blue flash.

I took out a sugar bowl from our family silver tea set and filled it half full of the rich brown island sugar and then, as an afterthought, for good luck, sprinkled some rice on top. I took a silver spoon. With these items in a bag, I tried not to run for the beach.

Back under the trees, I saw them come out of the sea. They must have been fifty yards from each other. My acquaintance Cole Robinson made for a spot on the beach. He picked up his towel, and I saw a standing flask. He looked over towards

Lydia drying off in the early breeze. He picked up the flask and he picked up two mugs. Gingerly, with some trepidation, I thought, he walked over towards her, and yet strongly and distinctly, I heard him ask:

"Coffee?"

Lydia froze for an instant. I knew she would. Trying to keep it in, I shook with mirth in my belly. She looked up into the large rhino face of my aquintance, and then graciously, obviously touched, she smiled and accepted. I could not believe it. I looked at the two of them standing there, beauty and beast with the early sun on their brown bodies. Oddly, they seemed quite enraptured with each other, smiling in that peculiar first meeting half-shy enraptured way.

I saw him give her a mug, open the flask, and start pouring the dark steaming liquid. His large hands were suprisingly steady and he now seemed quite sure of himself. Lydia, beautifully graceful, a smile composed now to a degree, as though she were hiding some great expectation, was just about to place the mug carefully to her lip when, bowl and spoon in hand, I swept out like a cavalier from under the trees.

"Sugar anybody?" was all I said. The rice eventually did the rest for brown sugar and rice are a small island love potion.

Colin Leslie Beadon of Barbados was born in Myanmar (formerly Burma) in 1935. He has lived in several countries. He writes: "The oilfields, sailing in West Indian waters, and writing have occupied much of my life." His stories have appeared in several magazines and been read on the BBC. He claims "to be a very obstinate typewriter basher" and that a loving aunt, an author herself, has been "my insistent inspiration."

"I hope you'll not do something
that you'll regret later."

Red Plum

BY KE ZHAOJIN

"FROM the States," my son, a strapping college student, said curtly, throwing a letter onto the desk at which I was translating an article for a scientific journal. I am a translator by profession, and that means I can stay home working most of the time. Without laying down my pen, I cast a glance at the envelope and immediately recognized the handwriting. It was surely from Red Plum, who had been my neighbor for about two years until a month ago. Eagerly I unsealed the letter and fished out the three thin sheets.

"Dear Mrs. Song,
    How time flies. At a mere wink of an eye one month has passed already. Well, first of all, I hope everything is all right with you..."

She was right; time certainly did fly. It seemed it had only been yesterday that we were still together. In my memory her image was fresh and vivid: a tall, slim, pretty girl with an unusually fair skin. She appeared very shy, but once she did look at you, you (even if you were a woman like me) would find yourself deeply drawn by her magnetic eyes. She had been a good woman, I thought, although she had been naïve and inexperienced in choosing her life partner. As I held the letter, my attention was diverted. What was it? As I searched for the answer, I found myself preoccupied by my first impression of her, a picture that was still so clear to me.

One day, two years ago, I was told that I could move into a room on the ground floor in a terraced house on Yuyuan Road. We, my son and I, were finally moving out of a room in the Shanghai Translation Press which we, so we were then told, had been occupying illegally for three years. Instead of thanking my boss, whose personal efforts were mainly responsible for my getting the room, I told him flat out that I did not like terraced houses since people there lived too close to each other and privacy was minimal. But my boss smiled patiently and asked me to take a look at the room assigned to me before making up my mind, and that very day, as soon as I left my office, I went to have a look at the room.

The place was easy to find. I was soon standing before the back door of the house bearing the number I had written down. It was in the middle of a row of similarly structured terraced houses, and as I surveyed their appearance, I could see instantly that these red-brick houses were much better in quality than I had imagined. Such houses usually had no gas, no W.C.; their wooden floors were heavily worn and their walls made not of bricks but wooden strips covered with mortar, with the result that the whole place was rat ridden. I reached out my hand and pressed the doorbell and I no sooner heard it ring inside than the door sprang open. A woman's sweet face popped out round the door, which she held open with one hand, while swinging her body behind the door.

"Are you looking for someone?" Her voice was soft, but by no means encouraging.

"I'm not looking for anybody in particuiar. I've come to see the house," I said matter-of-factly.

At this the face was quickly withdrawn and as the door opened further, a young woman, in her mid-twenties or thereabouts standing modestly by a gas stove, greeted me with a simple nod and a friendly sparkle in her extraordinarily bright eyes.

"I've been assigned the front room on the ground floor, and I'd like to have a look at it," I explained to justify my presence.

Actually I quite expected her to tell me something about the house by way of introduction, but she only smiled briefly and said, "You're welcome," before turning to attend to her cooking again.

I walked through the narrow passage along the wall on the right into the tiny courtyard, roofed in by a little square of blue sky. It was nice, I thought, and could hold many pot plants. The room itself was good, with brick walls and a large door with glass panes in the upper half of it. In spite of having to share the kitchen and the toilet, the room was nice enough for me to be satisfied immediately, and I moved in with my son the very next day.

Because I did most of my work at home, before the first week was out I had already learnt that the upstairs rooms were only occupied by one person—that young woman who had opened the door the day before and whom the postman would call to in his loud drawl, "Zhang Red Plum." She must surely be a brave woman to have lived all alone in this large house before I moved in. Red Plum and I had few dealings with each other, for she always seemed to leave home very early and come back well after suppertime. However, due to my initiative we managed to carry on some conversations, mostly monosyllabic on her part, through which I learnt that she was a graduate in Japanese from the Shanghai Institute of Foreign Languages, and was now working as a tourist guide for the Shanghai International Travel Service. It was a job that made many in the neighborhood look up to her. Red Plum, I noticed, was in fact a very beautiful young woman. She was very shapely, yet slender. In her oval face was set a pair of almond-shaped eyes, a straight nose and a sensuous mouth.

Her movements were graceful, and her mind intelligent and quick. With her elegance, her social position and her housing situation, it struck me that she must be one of the most marriageable young women in Shanghai. Did she have a boyfriend already? I wondered.

My question was soon answered. I was still in the kitchen one night when Red Plum came home very late. I heard her say good-bye to somebody and then a man's voice say, "I'll meet you at the same place at the same time. Good night." When Red Plum turned, she saw me and smiled shyly. She went upstairs without saying anything. Her life seemed very busy. She was absent from home even on Sundays, and I had little chance to have a long talk with her.

One Sunday morning she slept late and came down when I was already cooking lunch for my son and myself. She greeted me briefly and quickly cooked some noodles for her brunch, taking them upstairs to eat. A while later she came down again, not dressed to go out, but holding a basin of dirty clothes. I was glad to see her, thinking I could finally have a long talk with her while she did her laundry. To tell the truth, although the quietness of the house suited the nature of my work, I was bored with the increasingly solitary atmosphere of the house, in which I was virtually the only inhabitant, for my husband was working in Guangzhou, while my son who was studying at Fudan University came home only on weekends and Red Plum came home only to sleep. So I yearned for company and for some kind of social life, even on a very modest scale.

"Red Plum, are you the only one in your family?" I ventured, not sure if the question was too personal.

"No. I live with Huahua," she answered cheerfully. She seemed very happy that day.

"Huahua?" I looked at her in surprise.

"Oh, that's my bird, a canary. It's beautiful. It was given me by my boyfriend," she said, with a hint of pride.

I remembered that I had heard a bird chirping occasionally, but I had thought it the next-door neighbor's. So, she definitely did have a boyfriend. I said, "Anybody who is your boyfriend is really very lucky. With your advantages, you deserve to get the best young man in the whole of Shanghai."

"Mrs. Song, how did you guess? He is the best of the best, even if I do say it myself," she said, a big smile spreading over her face, such as I had never seen since I moved in. She was in a talkative mood and told me that her boyfriend was an artist, clever, handsome, and made a lot of money from his Chinese landscapes.

"I'm sure, you'll make a wonderful couple," I said. "Are you going to get married soon?"

"Maybe. Maybe not. It all depends on me. We've been going steady now for six month. Honestly, I quite like his personality. He is romantic, lively, animated, enthusiastic, and, most important, ambitious. He's asked me to marry him more than a dozen times already, but I've not given him my final word yet. He says he will buy the most expensive furniture from the Shanghai Furniture Shop, hold a large banquet in the Peace Hotel, and paint me—fourteen portraits—but I just told him that I was only interested in the character of the man I was going to marry and the other things were far less important. In fact, I've not decided yet if he is the right man to be my life companion."

"You mean you are not satisfied with him?" I asked.

"Well, I can't actually find any fault in him, but, but I still want to wait. He's coming here this afternoon. I'll arrange for you to meet each other so that you can tell me what you think." She looked lovely, smiling broadly.

I was washing up at the sink after lunch when the bell rang. After drying my hands on my apron, I opened the door to a young man around twenty-eight or twenty-nine. Knowing who it must be, I examined him carefully. He was tall, square-shouldered, with long hair. His complexion was very dark, and his thick brows and moustache were very black and conspicuous. He wore a checkered shirt shaped to fit a slim waistline, tucked into a pair of much-washed jeans. A huge canvas bag was slung across his shoulders. It amused me to note how well he put on the air of an artist. His whole appearance was rather unconventional. But weren't artists supposed to be unconventional, after all?

"I've come to see Zhang Red Plum," he said dramatically, smiling and showing his snow-white teeth. I felt rather embarrassed at having barred the doorway and scrutinized him for so long. "She's upstairs," I said quickly, and turned to call her. But Red Plum had already come down and was already standing beside me, her smile full of charm. She stepped forward and introduced the visitor to me. "This is Wang Gang, an artist in Chinese painting, and this is Mrs. Song, an artist in translation." I blushed. It's true that we translators like to think of ourselves as "artists," but the rest of the world thinks of us only as "hacks." Before I had a chance to explain about myself, Red Plum signaled with her large eyes, and the visitor brushed by me and followed her nimble footsteps quickly. They stayed upstairs till around five o'clock. After saying good-bye to her boyfriend, Red Plum joined me in the kitchen and began to cook her supper.

"Mrs. Song, he asked me to marry him again today," Red Plum began rather abruptly. "In fact, he asked me to marry him as soon as possible."

"Then what are you waiting for since you love him?" I asked bluntly while stirring my soup. I was cooking a lot of it, for my son was a heavy soup-eater.

"Mrs. Song, your question is hard to answer. The fact is I've been stalling because I don't want to be trapped. I don't want to have to divorce him later. It would cause a scandal. Actually, I've made up my mind. In fact, I made it up earlier this afternoon when he started staring at me yearningly." Red Plum suddenly looked serious.

"What have you decided?"

"I am not going to marry him and I will tell him through a third party that he should give up hoping to get me."

"But, but why?" I was surprised at my own tone of voice. Who was I to her anyway? Wasn't I being a bit officious?

"The answer is really quite simple. I don't want him to tie me down. I'm not stupid. If I know I'll be trapped, I'm going to swerve in time to avoid it! Now I'm convinced he is basically vulgar. He needs me not so much out of love as out of lust. Standing here, I can picture my future life with him. He's an artist. He'll paint, smoke, drink, boast, swear, complain, and ill-use me, while I will be nothing but a housewife, an object to satisfy his desire, and his personal secretary and servant. I will have to bear his child, wait on him, keep his house, run his errands, echo his word, console his whimsical soul, and do every menial thing just to make him happy! That's bondage, a system of slavery. I would be kept busy from morning till night, day in, day out, seven days a week! I would have no future of my own; no career of my own! I definitely don't want it!" She poured this out in a quick flow of words, as if she were not facing me, but the artist, her voice sounding hurt, her face pale.

When I asked her what she was going to do, she replied that she would break it off at once and find another boyfriend who would not make her picture all these terrible sights. But some days later the artist came again and made a scene. He yelled at her so loudly that I could hear him clearly while sitting at my desk:

"But you should have told me that you weren't interested in me months ago! Not today! You've wasted my time! An artist's time!"

Then I heard Red Plum answer back loudly and sharply, in a voice quite unlike her normally soft one. So they were quarreling! Then I heard what sounded like him slapping her face. This was followed by the artist storming downstairs and slamming the back door hard behind him. Red Plum staggered downstairs too, and fell into my arms. After a little cry, she smiled saying that it was good she had got rid of the brute. "Look how he boxed my ears. It would have been even worse if I married him," she said.

In a few days Red Plum was again elated. She had found a new boyfriend. I was not in the least surprised, knowing she was the kind of woman who would attract many suitors. As if to show him to me, several days later she brought him home. He was a sociology lecturer at Shanghai University, she told me. She had been attracted to him when she attended a lecture he gave one day at the Shanghai Municipal Workers Cultural Center. He was lecturing on the importance of cultural and intellectual life and the correct relationships between men and women in Chinese society. His eloquence, presentation, and wide knowledge captured her completely. After the lecture, she went up to the platform and asked him some questions. In this way they became acquainted. "He's very promising. He's only thirty-three, but he's published two books already. They are thinking of promoting him to associate professor," she told me very proudly as she was making coffee. I had not seen them come in, so when I began to ask questions about him, Red Plum called him down and introduced him. He was also tall, but spare, bespectacled, and rather stiff in his movements. My whole impression of him was that he had spent too much time reading or writing. He struck me as being rather obsequious, for as he shook hands warmly, he bent unnecessarily low. It was much too formal, specially in our kitchen, where I was standing in an apron by a gas stove, with my hands all greasy!

He began to come every week, always with a couple of books, magazines, or newspapers tucked under his arm. In my own room, I could hear his low, bass voice flowing fluently on and on as he talked to Red Plum endlessly, apparently giving her lessons in sociology. As a result, she began to talk to me in sociological and psychological jargon even in the kitchen, dropping remarks about Freudianism and existentialism, topics which were little known to me. But even as this was going on, I told myself, without any evidence, that Red Plum would spurn him once he ran out of things to lecture her on, or when he asked her to marry him. The reason was that hers was a character that was only keen on the unexpected, the new. Her education and experience would easily enable her to discover his shortcomings and way of doing things, and she would soon be able to picture what their married life would be like. That would sooner or later drive her to saying good-bye to him for good, just as she had done to his predecessor.

On the following Sunday it rained. I heard some light knocks on the door and opened it to find myself facing Red Plum's boyfriend. He looked pale, tired and bedraggled (he had no umbrella with him), as if he had trudged for miles without food or drink. Instead of books under his arms, he held only a handkerchief. "Is Red Plum in?" he asked in acute embarrassment. I nodded and let him in, smiling encouragingly. I watched him go upstairs hesitantly and at once guessed what had happened. Curious, I stood at the bottom of the stairs in the kitchen and listened attentively. There was no sound except the happy singing of Red Plum's canary Huahua. They must be talking in very low voices, I thought. This university lecturer was evidently a far cry from that artist in manliness. He must be very shy and timid in life, never daring to do anything not sanctioned by his social position—a future professor. But before long I heard Red Plum's high-pitched voice shouting:

"So you mean when a girl meets you, she must marry you even if you prove yourself a great disappointment? Do you mean it's God's will that I must love you and accept your proposal? I'm not in love with you. I know that from our meetings over the past three months. And three months is not short! Just leave like a gentleman and don't come back!"

I could tell from her voice that Red Plum was in her doorway and the university teacher had never entered the room.

"But I hope you will reconsider your rash decision. Please be sympathetic to my feelings. It's the first time I've ever fallen in love; you know in the past I was only absorbed in my study. If you jilt me, the blow will be too heavy! Maybe I do have faults, but just tell what they are so that I can correct them. Give me a chance."

The poor wretch's voice, imploring, was low and emotional. As I wondered if he would burst in tears, I heard Red Plum's voice again.

"Well, if you must know, you're too bookish. You can lecture on sociology all right, but that doesn't help you get along in life. Thousands of people who know nothing about sociology are stronger than you. How could I bear to live with you? You would read and talk about useless things all day long; pore over books and manuscripts every night; behave like an old man despite your age; you would be incapable of doing any housework and I would have to slave away with the household chores every day; you would't go out to the films, or concerts, or dances with me because you think they're a waste of time. You—you, you're a bookworm, out of place in the world! I'm not going to be trapped by you!" This speech was forcibly and bitingly delivered, followed by the slamming of her door.

The university teacher came down in very low spirits. He crossed the kitchen unsteadily, his face pensive, his jaw muscles tense. Afraid he would trip over the threshold, I hurried over to open the door for him. It was still raining, for it was already approaching mid-autumn. I watched him stagger on crestfallen along the narrow lane until he disappeared behind a corner.

Red Plum came downstairs for some water. She smiled at me awkwardly and explained, "My God, it's hard to find a good boyfriend these days. If you don't like them after a while, they refuse to go, and are just like leeches! Well, I wonder if I shall find another one soon."

Intuitively I knew she would, perhaps a boyfriend of a rarer nature since she was fed up with the common run. Having lived with her in the same house for months, I was sure she had no women friends and went about with men.

Besides, her physical charms and unique qualities would certainly enable her to catch another heart with ease.

One evening weeks later she came back wearing a pair of new leather shoes, which were obviously not made in China. She stood before me and clicked her heels. "How do you like them?" She asked, beaming. "Have you got a new boyfriend?" I asked. "Not exactly," she began to explain. She had made friends with a Chinese from America, a Mr. K, and found him very exciting. "He work's for a company in New York. He's over fifty but looks much younger. He came back for his brother's funeral. That was a fortnight ago. Now he's womanizing in Shanghai before going home."

"You mean he's sleeping with our virgins for chicken fees?" I asked in alarm, having heard what some returned overseas Chinese were up to.

"I can't prove anything. But that's what I have been told. Anyway, there are plenty who are willing to be taken advantage of," she said quietly.

"How do you know?"

"Easy. Just go and look at some of the girls in the bars and restaurants in the big hotels. They sit there curious and inquisitive, staring at everything around them. Ordinary Chinese can't get into the big hotels, and if they were the relatives of the overseas Chinese they would have been to the bars and restaurants so many times they wouldn't look surprised and curious. On my job I often see girls like that." I was astonished, but Red Plum was not finished yet. "They say that those overseas Chinese are so stingy, they pay only twenty *yuan* a time. You know that's terribly cheap compared with what they pay in the West," Red Plum whispered.

I was shocked; also I had not thought that Red Plum was a girl who could have told me what she just had. I kept my eyes averted and said, "You're getting off the point, Red Plum."

"Oh, yes, Mr. K. He's old enough to be my father, but still he looks stronger than that university teacher of mine. But he always avoids telling me too much about himself. There's something mysterious about him, and he seems to have something within him that draws you to him." Here she lowered her voice although there was not another soul in the whole house, and added, "I think I'm in love with him already. I don't know why."

"Maybe because he's from America," I remarked lightly.

"Oh, Mrs. Song, don't say that! In fact, I can never marry him because of his age and in any case he's married. I just like him, that's all. He's taken me out a couple of times and bought me this pair of shoes." She indicated them by a nod. "Anyway, he's leaving next week for New York. I'm planning to invite him here before he goes, so that you may see for yourself how out of the ordinary he is."

The following day was Sunday, and Red Plum came with Mr. K. The taxi drove into the lane and stopped before the back door. (It was quite a job for the driver to back the car out.) It was about ten in the morning, a time when many doors were open. I was washing—as I did every Sunday morning—but was called by Red Plum the moment they stepped into the kitchen. She wanted to introduce Mr. K. She took her time, evidently to give me enough time to examine her guest. I glanced at the man and thought he was dressed in a rather juvenile fashion: striped shirt with "I love you" printed on the front, the tail of which was tucked inside a pair of trousers with many pockets; on his feet he had on a pair of milk-colored leather shoes with sharp toes. I looked up at his face. He must have been very handsome in his day. But now his temples had turned gray, his eyes peered from behind a pair of gold-rimmed glasses, and his hair was oiled and well combed. He seemed a rich overseas Chinese who could have been educated at some posh university. He greeted me very politely in the perfect Shanghai dialect (which actually sounded a bit old-fashioned and a bit aristocratic) and shook hands warmly.

They stayed upstairs for a long time, during which I frequently heard Red plum giggling. That man indeed had made a hit with her. They did not have lunch and left around two in the afternoon. Next morning I got up early as usual to do shadow boxing in my small courtyard. For one movement I had my arms akimbo as I shook my neck. It happened I was looking up when the window upstairs opened and out popped Red Plum's head. She was looking at the weather for it was very important to her as a tourist guide. She had told me that she never did quite trust the weather forecast on Radio Shanghai. To my surprise, I also saw another head with sleek hair and the flash of glasses. So Mr. K had stayed overnight! Funny. When had he come back? Had he sneaked in after I had gone to bed?

"He was here last night?" I asked Red Plum that night in the kitchen, emphasizing the word "here" so that she surely could catch the implication. At the same time I was surprised to note that I had taken it upon myself to look after her morals. (Was it just because I was her senior or because she had no parents?) I remembered that at my work place I had been known as "a woman who didn't interfere in the business of others."

"Yes, I asked him to stay here although we could have stayed in his hotel room," she answered frankly.

I was astonished at her straightforwardness. "But why didn't you go to his room? It must be much more comfortable," I pursued rather sarcastically.

"Oh, I would never do that. The waiters there all know me," she said with a faint smile that was tinged with satisfaction.

While she had the cheek to banter with me, I did not have the courage to ask her any other questions. As I turned to go to my own room, I said over my shoulder, "I hope you'll not do something that you'll regret later."

"I won't, Mrs. Song."

Although Mr. K had left China many days before, Red Plum never stopped talking about him. She missed him dreadfully. Then, one day when I was in the kitchen she came to me and said she felt sick and asked me if I had any pills to calm her stomach. Even as she was making the request, she bent down, trying to vomit. Nothing came up. From my experience I immediately guessed that she was pregnant.

"You are in trouble," I said sternly. "You're expecting."

"Expecting? Why, that's wonderful! How wonderful!" she exclaimed excitedly instead of feeling frightened.

I was more than surprised and thought she must have gone mad. "What a bastard Mr. K is to leave you in such a mess!"

"Oh, don't blame him. It's I who seduced him. I want to have a child by him so that I can have him eventually."

"But—but why? I thought you told me he was a married man?" I was very flustered.

"He doesn't get along with his present wife. He'll divorce her, just as he divorced his two former wives in the past!"

"What a rascal! I know the type. He was kind to you just so he could sleep with you! He's clean forgotten you by now!"

"It's not like that at all! You don't understand him, but I do even though I stayed with him only briefly. He divorced his former wives because they failed to understand him."

I was stunned. What could I do to make her see the truth? How could she, who had stayed with him only briefly, understand him, a worldwise, sophisticated man who was old enough to be her father? How could she, who looked with disdain at handsome young men of her own age, have fallen in love with an aging man like that? I couldn't find the answer. Perhaps it is true that love is blind!

I asked her what she was going to do. She had to face reality. She replied with firmness she was going to write to Mr. K and tell him the good news. She would urge him to divorce his present wife and marry her. I said that was too cruel and immoral, but Red Plum said that she did not care since love was selfish and Mr. K was not happy with his wife now. A month later Red Plum told me triumphantly that Mr. K had written to her saying that his wife had agreed to divorce him on condition that he left his house to her. He said he was going to be as free as a bird again and would fly in to marry her.

"Exactly what is it that makes you so infatuated with him?" I asked her again.

"I don't think I can give you or even myself a satisfactory answer. He has something in him that draws me to him. I know if I marry him, he'll lead me into some wonderful, indescribable life," she said, her eyes half-closed as if half-hypnotized.

"I suddenly realized Red Plum was in search of the unexpected and unimaginable. Mr. K had captured her heart and soul simply because he had offered her a vague picture of himself and of their future. But what would happen when Red Plum married him and the picture became clear and the illusions vanished? She would be disappointed and full of regret! Then...I did not dare to think further. It was senseless to do so, for now she was bearing his child and determined to marry him.

Like many married women, Red Plum was no longer shy about things concerning relationships between men and women. In fact, she became direct and bold on the subject. When her belly was conspicuous enough, her bosses, three men, came one day. In her room, they talked loudly, trying to insist she have an abortion since the child would be illegitimate. "But I said my child was perfectly legitimate. It had the right to be born. His father was in the United States, going through the necessary formalities for marrying me. He was coming to Shanghai and we would soon be husband and wife officially," Red Plum told me as soon as the three men had gone. "But actually I'm not sure when Mr. K will come. I wonder what I'll do if he doesn't turn up when I'm about to give birth. But, I guess when the child is too large, they won't be able to force me to have an abortion and so I'll have it in the end!" she said.

As her pregnancy advanced, Red Plum began to take more and more days off from her work. (She had already been transferred to work in an office which arranged tickets for tourists.) She had become more talkative, and we had many opportunities for conversations because of her being at home more often. One day she was so cheerful that she took her bird to the kitchen to bathe it. As she splashed water on it, the bird hopped lively in the cage and warbled merrily. "Look how happy the water makes the bird," she remarked. "I need Mr. K to make me happy." She was talking more to herself than to me—I was cleaning my gas stove. "I've led a very miserable life since my mother died of cancer in 1970. I have never seen my father. My mother always refused to talk about him, I don't know why. After my mother died, I was looked after by an uncle who emigrated to Canada recently." She paused, gazing at the bird which was now busily preening its feathers. "It's interesting to think that I'm going to be looked after by Mr. K," she said gaily.

I listened but made no comment. In my mind I was rather worried about her, for she had as yet learnt nothing from life and was being silly.

Time flew. I watched Red Plum's belly swell day by day. Before long she was in her ninth month. Mr. K was not quite as wicked as I had thought. He had posted money to her every month so that starting with her fifth month of pregnancy she had been employing a maid. However, I very much doubted if Mr. K would show up when the time came for her to give birth. "But I'm sure he will be here," Red Plum repeatedly assured me.

I was proven right. But since she had her maid, things were not as difficult as they might have been. When the child was three months old, Mr. K suddenly appeared, saying he had finally divorced his wife and had come to marry her. Red Plum was elated. She threw herself into Mr. K's arms, weeping and smiling at the same time. Looking at this scene taking place in the kitchen, I was reminded of the movies in which the heroines had done the same thing when united with their beloved husbands after a separation of thirty years or something. I do not know how she got through the marriage registration since she had already had a son, but when they came back in a taxi, Red Plum's face was radiant. Mr. K stayed in our house with Red Plum and behaved like a good house husband. Smiling continually, he would help the maid do many things and would negotiate the sixteen steps frequently from morning till night carrying things upstairs and downstairs.

Partially out of curiosity and partially out of my concern for Red Plum, I decided to find an opportunity to have a good talk with him to learn more about his personality and if he really was able to support his wife and son. But before I had a chance to do so, he disappeared. I had heard Mr. K leave through the back door the previous night, but had not known he was heading for Hongqiao Airport.

"So your Mr. K left suddenly, after staying only a fortnight?" I asked Red Plum on the morrow.

Red Plum was pacing in the kitchen, with her child in her arms. She answered, "His company wanted him for something urgent. He had to go. But he'll be back when I fly to New York with my son."

"So you are leaving too?" I asked, feeling an abrupt sense of sadness at the thought of her leaving me probably for good. I had already become attached to her.

"Yes," Red Plum answered, her eyes gleaming with joy.

A couple of months later a letter came from the American Embassy in Beijing, informing her that she and her son's immigration had been approved. Mr. K did not come back. He sent her a Pan-American ticket and said he would meet her at Kennedy Airport. I saw Red Plum and her child off at the airport. She was reluctant to part from me and said she would miss me a lot. She trusted her home to my care and promised to come back to Shanghai to see me and her native place in one or two years' time. The parting caused us both to shed many tears.

I realized I had been holding Red Plum's letter a long

while without reading it. I smoothed it on my desk, stopped reminiscing and began to read:

"Dear Mrs. Song,

How time flies. At a mere wink of an eye one month has passed already. Well, first of all, I hope everything is all right with you..."

I skipped some paragraphs quickly to read:

"Instead of finding myself more and more at home, I find myself more and more a stranger. I don't speak the language, and so I can't find a job. I'm nothing but a combination of housewife, baby-sitter, and sex object for Mr. K. I'm shut in all day like the caged canary in my old home, but unlike it, I don't sing, only cry. So far I've not made a single friend. Mr. K often comes home very late and sometimes he doesn't come home at all. He says that it's his job, but I've already guessed that he doesn't work for a company at all and is just an odd-job man. He leads a loose life, I think, and from time to time I receive calls from women speaking in English which I don't understand. When I ask him to explain, he always says they are his business associates. He has already warned me not to interfere too much with his life! Even worse, he smokes like a chimney and drinks like a fish. He often uses filthy language and pays little attention to our son. I now understand·why his former wives all left him! In fact, I'm suffering terribly, and the air here is smothering me to death. As I think of this, oh how I wish I were in my old house with you!... Mrs. Song, do you remember I once told you for fun that I would marry a man whose actions I could not predict? Mr. K is certainly ideal in this respect. I'm totally ignorant of what his next move will be! If you ask me if Mr. K loves me, my answer is I don't know; if you ask me if he will divorce me someday, my answer is again I don't know. There are too many things about him I don't know! I don't know exactly what his job is, what he does when he stays out overnight, how much he earns, what his past was, if he will lose his temper and beat me, what his philosophy of life is...The pigeon holes I have in my mind to hold information about him are empty. I can't learn anything with which to fill them. He never tells me the truth. He smirks and hems and haws all the time...Mrs. Song, you are always very kind to me. Please write to comfort me and tell me what to do. I have been naïve and need help...Finally, I also miss my Huahua. Please set him free immediately..."

What help could I give her since we were separated by the vast Pacific Ocean and since I knew so little about life in New York? Although I could offer no advice, I forced myself to write to her immediately to comfort her. That I could do. There was something else for me to do. Huahua was chirping upstairs; it was time I set him free. I wished he would fly to his mistress and cheer her up just a little.

Born in Shanghai, in 1954, Ke Zhaojin attended the Shanghai Institute of Foreign Languages from which he earned his BA and MA degrees. He has been a special correspondent for China Daily *and now teaches English literature on the university level and writes short fiction.*

"Noticing the astonished expression on my face,
the manager obviously concluded that
I was scared..."

Wednesday Morning:
a Christmas
Conspiracy Tale

BY IVAN KLÍMA

ON Wednesday morning, the day before Christmas, I got up at a quarter past four. Although I had set the alarm for five o'clock, the thought of having to get up so damnably early had kept me awake since three. I shuffled off to the dining room, which had a north-facing window, on whose frame was mounted a thermometer. Pointing my flashlight at the scale, I saw that it registered only a fraction above freezing. Cold enough for me not to relish the prospect of spending eight or nine hours out in the open, standing up and with my hands forever immersed in cold water. Still, it wasn't too bad for the time of year, so I should not really bewail my fate—it could have been much colder.

The kids were asleep, my wife too, and so I made my own breakfast and ate it in the kitchen. Then I put on two pullovers, a windcheater, and three pairs of socks. After yesterday's experience I would have preferred four, but my boots were too small for that.

I had been inveigled into this whole business by Peter, a former colleague of mine from the faculty. Peter was a lecturer in aesthetics, a literary critic and philologist. These past three years, however, he had been earning a living first as a night watchman in the warehouse of some building firm, and then as a stoker. During that time he had spent all his savings and, having discovered that it was impossible to keep body and soul together by honest toil, had decided to chuck it in and seek a more lucrative way of life.

I had not heard from him for at least half a year, and then he phoned me a week ago; after the usual questions about my health and work came a matter-of-fact query: "How would you like to sell fish?"

"How would I like *what*...?"

"Sell carp for Christmas," he explained "You can earn a heap of money doing that."

"Oh but I..." The proposal was so unexpected that I completely missed my opportunity to refuse. "Well, I must say that's something I've never thought of doing."

"Of course you haven't," he said reassuringly. "Who would have? But you're a writer—you should try your hand at everything."

"I'm not the kind of writer who has to try everything," I countered.

"Sure you are!" he replied, his voice tinged with the authority of his former calling. "Anyway, you'll make a lot of money. You're not going to tell me you couldn't use it, now that Christmas is coming."

"But look, I've never killed a carp in my life. I just couldn't do it," I added, hoping that this would be the end of the matter.

"Oh, don't worry about that side of it," he said. "Leave that to me. And that apart, it's child's play. Two or three days, that's all, and you can expect to take home at least two thou."

An hour later he was at my apartment, to continue his enthusiastic depiction of the job he wanted me to undertake. Last year, one of his former students had sold carp outside the White Swan department store, and in four days had earned ten thousand, tax-free. And even if we did not manage to get as good a venue—because that would obviously cost us—we'd still be sure to make two or three thousand at the very least. Of course, he explained, if we wanted a decent spot we would first have to grease somebody's palm.

At last I realized what he was after. He had a splendid idea, he was willing to put in some hard work himself and even to slaughter the carp, but he needed a partner with some capital.

"How much?" I asked him.

Peter had a squint. Now, too, each of his eyes was looking in a different direction. What I found suspicious was that neither was looking at me.

"Well...how much?"

"Say five hundred for the spot," he replied, "a hundred for the fish warden, and a bottle of brandy for the manager of the supermarket in front of which we'll do the selling."

"That's quite an investment," I pointed out.

"The more we put in, the more we'll make," he assured me. "And I've found a fantastic spot in Strašnice."

"What's that with the fish warden?"

He explained that if you wanted to make a profit you had to have decent fish. That former student of his—who had made enough money selling carp outside the White Swan to pay for a trip to India—had told him about some fellow who had ignored the fish warden. The fish warden had then simply called out, "Fish for Mr. Scrooge!" and the soldiers opened a different tank, out of which came carp that looked more like minnows.

"Soldiers?" I asked, puzzled by this new element in the transaction. *"What* soldiers?"

"Why, those manning the fish tanks, of course," he replied somewhat uncertainly. "They tell me there are soldiers there. So what."

I did not share his confidence where the soldiers were concerned, but if the truth were told, it wasn't the eight hundred crowns he was asking that put me off. I simply did not fancy the idea of standing there in the street from morning till night next to a tank full of carp. In any case, I didn't particularly need the money, I had enough to live on and a little in the savings bank. Things being as they were I could hardly expect to be earning more. So I was not really interested in this extra cash, I wouldn't know what to do with it, unless I donated it to somebody. If you are willing to hand money out, you can never have enough. But for *that* purpose two thousand was a ridiculous amount.

True, a number of my friends were in jail, all of them dangerous subversives and conspirators, if you were to believe the indictment. That they should be cooling their heels in prison while we others were enjoying a degree of freedom which even allowed us to choose whether we wished to sell carp was all part of the Russian roulette that fate had been playing with us for some thirty years.

One of those in prison had been a colleague of mine in the editorial office of a literary magazine in the days when these were still being published in this country. Christmas would be just the right time to pay his wife a visit and bring her a little money.

I lent Peter that eight hundred. He left in high spirits, promising to see to everything, fish included.

At a quarter to five I was ready. I had washed, shaved, breakfasted, put on three pairs of socks and a pair of boots. Now I tried reading the sports page of yesterday's newspaper, but there is not much in the way of sports going on around Christmas, and we all know that there is nothing of interest in the rest of the paper at any time of year.

At five I emerged into the frosty morning. The thin mist smelled of smoke, sulphur, and bad humor. Soon we'll all choke and become extinct, just as we have poisoned the fish in most of our rivers. All we are left with are some bemused carp in a few select ponds.

Yesterday was our first day as fish salesmen. We reached the agreed spot in complete darkness. The carp, which Peter had procured the day before, filled a huge tank standing in front of the dimly lit supermarket; its manager, a portly, graying, elegantly attired fellow, gave us a friendly greeting, his friendship having previously been secured with a bottle of brandy. He gave us a hand with the wooden counter we brought out of the storeroom, and then he dragged out an ancient-looking pair of scales. For a while he looked on, amused, as we attempted to align the scales on this complicated contraption, then he pushed us out of the way and, after making some fine adjustments, jovially assured us that it could now be relied on to give us five percent extra per kilogram. He further instructed us never to fail throwing the fish on the scales with the maximum quantity of water—"tip the water out only if the customer has looked at the scales beforehand"—then snatch the carp away as soon as the indicator reaches the highest point, making sure at the same time that the scales should not ever show a whole, easily read weight such as one or one-and-a-half kilos. We listened most attentively, which encouraged him to give us some more useful hints. Naturally, it went without saying that we had to round the price up to the nearest whole number, if possible to the number nine, which was the best of all whole numbers. Then throw in a few odd pence on top, as that made it look more convincing. By way of example the manager thrust his hand in the tank, fished out a carp and threw it on to the recently adjusted scales. One kilogram nineteen crowns, then add a few pence for the sake of appearances—say, nineteen crowns sixty. Customers as a rule pay with a large denomination note and don't expect any small change. That gives us an acceptable price of twenty crowns. However, the manager continued our initiation with evident glee, it can happen that a somewhat absent-minded customer enables you to quote an even higher price, like twenty crowns twenty. In that case always demand your change back. If this proves difficult, you can show magnanimity by saying, "Never mind, you keep the change—I'll collect it next Christmas!" Not only does that look good, the customer will usually demur and tip you a crown or two extra, *on top* of the twenty. You can thus make three or four crowns on a seventeen-crown carp, taking into account what you already gained on the scales.

Noticing the astonished expression on my face, the manager obviously concluded that I was scared, and so he turned to me and assured me there was nothing to be afraid of. Most of the customers were women, who hardly ever noticed what the weight was, much less were able to calculate the price. But of course it was up to me to be skilful and to use psychology: to sum up the customer, chat her up a bit so that she forgets she is out shopping but feels she is making a date. And therefore, men, beware of men! All this, the manager imparted to us with a faint smile on his lips, as if he was not being serious but just joking, merely playacting for our benefit.

"However, as soon as you mention the price you have to be serious again. Sometimes it helps to apologize and say you've got it wrong, correcting the price in the customer's favor."

He pointed to the scales, with the seventeen-crown carp still writhing on top of them, giving us a graphic demonstration of what he had in mind. "That'll be twenty-three sixty, madam," he said, picking up the writhing fish and turning towards me, carp in hand. "Oh, I *beg* your pardon! Just one moment, please." He threw the carp back on the scales, only to snatch it off again, his face assuming so penitent an expression that to harbor any doubt about the sincerity of his apology or to defile that moment of truth by indulging in something as base as addition or subtraction would have been to offend his integrity as a salesman and his dignity as a human being. "There," he cried, "I almost cheated you, madam. It's only twenty-two crowns ten." And with these words the manager hurled the unfortunate carp back into the tank, packed with its fellow-victims which kept opening their stupid mouths, as Nature intended, oblivious to the coins clinking in their throats for the sake of which they would shortly be fished out, slaughtered, fraudulently overpriced, and eventually eaten.

I got off the half-empty bus. It was only half-past five, which meant I had added an extra thirty minutes to the inevitable eight hours of freezing. The street was deserted, except for a few sleepy, obviously irritable pedestrians. From afar I could see our tank. The day before had not been a raging success, businesswise. Although women had trooped into the supermarket by the dozen, buying up everything from sugar to soap powder as if bereft of reason, to our dismay they appeared to be in no hurry to purchase their Christmas carp, perhaps because they had no room left in their bulging shopping bags; and so we froze outside the store for nothing. It was not till almost lunchtime that a few old-age pensioners and housewives took any interest in what we had to offer. I did the weighing and collected the money while Peter doubled as fisherman-murderer. He handed me the still seemingly live bodies, which I would cautiously place on the scales.

The old ladies looked on trustingly, while the younger women exchanged a few sentences, some even flirted with me a little, so that I all but forgot that I was there to sell fish and not to make assignations. While engaged in all this chatter, I had my work cut out just converting grams into crowns—as for any rounding up, I lacked the necessary gall, cynicism and mental agility.

The women left and we were alone again. And cold. Peter started telling me all about Hasek's materialism and anarchism but then—doubtless influenced by the tankful of animal life at our side—quickly switched to animal symbolism in the works of Franz Kafka. He pointed out that with Kafka, man could always change into an animal, but never the other way round. In his view, the animal is invariably something repulsive, foul, slimy—a mouse, a mole, a monkey, even an insect. Peter could not say whether this included fish.

We carried on this conversation for a while, but it was too elevated a topic for those freezing conditions. We therefore played at being conspirators and succeeded (exactly how and by what means we did not for the moment specify) in forcing the government to obey our instructions. We ordered the immediate release of all political prisoners and restricted police powers to such a degree that they became practically nonexistent. We agreed that we would not put anyone on trial, and thus do away, once and for all, with the unending cycle of retribution which only created new victims. And finally, how else, we set about drawing up editorial programs—naturally consisting entirely of banned authors. We ended up with some eighty titles, whereas the total of carp we had managed to sell was eight. Not nearly so encouraging as the outcome of our conspiratorial activity.

At two o'clock we "shut up shop" for thirty minutes, adjourning for a hot cup of tea with rum to the storeroom at the rear of the supermarket. It was prepared for us on the manager's orders by one of the three young shop assistants who answered to the somewhat exotic name of Daniela. Her face, though, was typically Slav, her small nose flattened Russian-style, her hair probably a little reddish but you could not tell because she had recently had it dyed yellow, no doubt with a view to the approach of Christmas.

We sipped our tea, Miss Daniela sipping with us. Holding the mug in her tiny flippers, she looked quite delectable. She was generous with the rum, and so we felt very cosy with her in that storeroom at the rear of the shop. My friend, in keeping with his former vocation, recounted stories about famous writers while I, when asked to contribute to the entertainment, told them about my meeting with a former President. I don't think his name meant anything to the young lady from the supermarket, but she seemed quite thrilled to be rubbing shoulders with someone who had, in his turn, rubbed shoulders with a President. She kept eyeing me with what she no doubt considered provocative glances.

Arriving at our stall next day, the first thing I saw was the enormous pool of water licking the sides of the tank. I waded through it on tiptoe and, fearing the worst, looked inside.

Countless open fish mouths gaped at me from among the mass of carp bodies in that waterless container, some of the expiring bodies still twitching in their death throes.

I was seized with panic. There must have been a good eight thousand crowns' worth of fish in there. In all his calculations, Peter had never made any mention of the possibility of their total extinction. Quick as a flash I wondered if I had in any way been responsible for the catastrophe, but I could not think of anything I had done wrong or neglected to do. Then, stripping off my windcheater and rolling up the sleeves of both my pullovers—and doing my best to overcome my revulsion—I thrust my arm into the welter of twitching bodies. It did not take me long to locate the aperture through which the water had escaped, but it was at least another quarter of an hour (or so it seemed to me) before I found the plug. At last I did discover it under that mountain of fish and wedged it into the opening with all the strength I could muster. Any water that might still have remained in the tank would now no longer run out.

The trouble was, I had no means of filling the tank up again. Finding a paper cup in the waste bin I tried to scoop up some water from the pool on the pavement, but it was hopeless.

I threw away the cup and ran into the building that housed our supermarket. At this hour, naturally, it was closed. I crept past the doors of the apartments, trying to detect signs of life inside.

With the exception of the postman delivering a telegram, only *they* can ring a stranger's doorbell at six a.m. when they come to make an arrest. Only now did it occur to me that anyone in that line of work had to be quite shameless and thick-skinned.

I ran down to the cellar in the hope of finding a laundry room.

I did find a laundry room. From behind the locked door I could even hear a tap dripping. Taking my bunch of keys from my pocket I tried in vain to open the door. The thought of those dying carp lent me courage and I lunged at the door with my shoulder, kicking it several times for good measure.

The sound of footsteps up above startled me. I had enough to contend with already without being accused of hooliganism.

As I made my way backstairs I saw yellow-haired Daniela tripping towards the tank with a bucket of water in her hand. "These rotten tanks," she said by way of explanation. "Everything around here is rotten. Our freezers go on the blink at least once a month, usually on a Sunday. Come Monday morning we've got ice cream pastries and spinach running all over the floors. The burglar alarm goes off if somebody just *walks* past the shop window in the evening and it'll ring like mad, fit to wake the dead. Then the cops turn up and get the manager out of bed to check if anything's been taken."

We kept bringing bucketfuls of water to the tank, Daniela complaining all the while about the rotten supermarket where a person could not earn a penny on the side because all the goods came already packaged and weighed. Coffee was the only commodity you could make a *little* profit on, but for that you again had to have empty bags. She recalled her predecessor, who got hold of some Tuzex bags, which she filled with the coffee that was left under the grinder; she patiently filled the black Tuzex Special bags and took these all the way to Vršovice, where she sold them door-to-door, both for Czech crowns and for Tuzex coupons. With her coupons she bought genuine Scotch, which she then sold here at the store, making some two hundred crowns per bottle. In the end someone had ratted on her and she had to go, being posted to a pharmacy in Hostivař. Instead of coffee, she now had plaster-of-Paris to weigh, and instead of whisky she sold genuine South Bohemian wine.

By the time my friend and the cause of all my misfortune turned up, there was enough water in the tank for some of the fish bodies to turn their bellies heavenward and so demonstrate their pitiful demise.

We dumped all the corpses into a bucket, and as soon as the manager arrived went to ask him what to do with them so as not to infringe any hygiene regulations.

He glanced inside the bucket without the least sign of surprise, as if it had been he himself who had taken the plug out during the night. "How many?" he asked.

"Sixteen, I'd say," replied my friend. (Actually there were twenty, but I suppose Peter thought that by quoting a lower figure he would minimize our fiasco.)

"You'd *say*?" the manager repeated mockingly. "And now you'll want to throw them out, no doubt?"

"Well, what else?"

Astonishment at last showed in the manager's face. "What else? What *else*? Why, we'll gut them, cut them up into portions, and sell them at a higher price, of course."

And so I found myself in the warm and intimate atmosphere of the storeroom. With an apron, a butcher's knife, and the yellow-haired Daniela to help me, I stood over a much-used bench right at the back, hidden from the eyes of the world behind boxes full of sunflower oil bottles, to put the dead fish to good use.

It was a large storeroom, which smelled of spice and soap powder. In the corner opposite, a huge wooden crate with a hinged top attracted my attention. I had no idea what kind of merchandise it could be used for.

Miss Dana squeezed between me and the wall of boxes. Lightly brushing against my back with her breasts, she gave a delighted giggle and said wasn't it a scream to be given such a cushy job for a change.

I had never gutted a fish in my life, and so I watched attentively as her gentle fingers grasped the knife, cut open the gray body of the carp, and carefully extracted the innards.

"What do you do normally?" she asked. "Last Christmas we had a bunch of students here—but you're not a student, are you?"

"No, it's many years since I was a student."

"What you said yesterday about the President, remember? That was a lot of codswallop, wasn't it?"

"No."

"No?"

"No."

"Cross your heart?"

"No really!"

"Would you believe it!" She threw the portions of fish into a tin bowl. "What do they call you?"

"Ivan."

"That's not much of a name, is it?"

"Well, I suppose they didn't think so when they gave it to me."

"Not that I think much of *my* name," she admitted.

"What name would you prefer, then?"

"Lucia. Isn't that a lovely name? Lucia Masopustová," she replied in a dreamy voice.

"Otherwise you're happy?"

"What do you mean, otherwise?"

"With your lot."

The word "lot" seemed to amuse her. "Go on with you," she said, going over to the washbasin to rinse her hands. Then she pulled a chair across, sat down, and took a packet of cigarettes from her coat pocket. She offered me one, but I refused it, saying I didn't smoke. "Well, you can at least sit down, can't you." She took a wooden box down from the pile and placed it opposite her chair. "I don't have to tell you I'd much rather work in a greengrocer's or a gas station." She crossed her legs, shortening the distance between us. Although our legs did not touch, a mouse could not have squeezed through the space between them. It was obviously up to me to eliminate the space altogether. "Go on," I said. "Wouldn't you mind the fumes?"

"Mind? Have you any idea how much you can make in a month?"

"No," I confessed.

"Ten thousand, if it's a halfway decent pump. Eight at the very least."

"You're kidding," I said in disbelief. "Anyway, what would you do with all that money?"

"Lord Almighty!" she exclaimed, "You'd be surprised."

"All right, then why *don't* you work at a gas station?"

"Are you being funny?" She gave me a look full of contempt. Just then I heard a door squeak and then the voice of the manager. "Dana!" he shouted "What's with those fish? Let's have some portions over here!"

Miss Daniela leapt from her chair, put out her cigarette, grabbed the tin bowl with six halves of carp, and made for the door.

I got up, picked up the next deceased and cut his belly open. I was itching to find out how Peter was doing outside, but I did not fancy leaving my warm haven. I would have to go out there before too long, though—it was hardly fair to leave a friend to freeze out in the street while I chatted up the shop assistant.

Daniela came back. "He says we'd better get a move on. There's a bunch of old ladies waiting."

"I'm doing all I can."

"That's all right," she said. "Fuck 'em."

And with this she resumed our previous conversation. "If it was that easy, everybody would be working at the gas stations. D'ya know how much I'd have to cough up? Twenty-five thousand at least—and *then* they'd put me in the storeroom for a year, where I'd earn bugger-all. And what if after that they give me the boot? Or if the boss whose palm I'd greased gets the elbow? I'd have to pay up all over again."

"So what about the greengrocer's?" I asked.

"It's all the same," she said dejectedly, cutting open another corpse. "You didn't get *here* for nothing, did you?"

She looked up at me.

"No, I didn't."

"What do you do for a living?"

"Guess!"

"How should I know. You're not a student, and you don't work with your hands. Maybe you've been in the jug?"

I shrugged.

"I see," she said, nodding to show she understood.

"What charge would you say?"

"Charge? You mean why they put you inside?"

"That's right."

"Black market?" she ventured.

"No."

"Embezzlement?"

"No."

"Or did you open your mouth in the pub and say something you shouldn't have?"

"Well..." I said noncommittally. I don't like telling lies.

"What did they give you?"

"Doesn't matter," I said, closing the subject with a wave of my hand.

"I know," she said. "My elder sister got two years hard labor. She used to work at a railway station. And she didn't do nothing, either. Just because she knew about the pilfering that went on. My dad did six years, but I don't remember nothing about that, I had only just been born. *He* did time because he had owned a shop. When he came out he said to us: 'I never stole a bean in my life, and let me tell you, I was a damned fool!'"

"What does your father do now?"

"He's retired," she said. "Before that he was in charge of a canteen. But he never learned the ropes. My parents just didn't know the score." She threw another gutted fish in the bowl and went on: "You know who *does* know the ropes? Him over there," she pointed toward the shop. "Our manager. F'r instance, he used to transport the meat from the slaughterhouse in Budějovice. They always dropped off a quarter of the load for themselves and delivered the rest. But then the others got greedy and wanted to split it half and half. Well, our boss knows better than that, he knows when it's better to call it a day. So he moved, while his chums carried on for another year, and then went mad and started buying houses and posh foreign cars and they all landed up behind bars. By that time our manager was here in Prague, delivering beer in cahoots with a guy at the brewery, but again he wouldn't dream of taking too much, he was too clever for that. Just a few cases from each truckload. But that was enough to give them each a hundred a day. And then he got fed up driving all the time and got the job here in the supermarket. He's been here five years now and d'ya think he's had a deficit in all that time? Not on your life!" She raised her forefinger to emphasize the absence of a deficit under her boss's management. "He's got everybody bribed up at head office, and so he always knows a week in advance when a stocktaking is due, so they can never catch him by surprise. *And* he keeps in with us, too," she concluded her eulogy.

"Want some more tea?" she asked. "I guess your friend might like some, too."

On her way to the stove she again had to pass between me and the boxes that formed a high wall behind my back. I leaned backwards and felt her soft body trapped in the narrow space.

"Oh, Mr. Ivan!" I heard her protest softly. "What're you up to?"

Now I suppose I should have turned swiftly and kissed her. But what then? And in any case my hands were covered in carp blood, and for some reason it seemed inappropriate to wipe them on my apron as a prelude to an amorous gambit. Before I could decide what to do, much less do it, I felt her moist girlish breath on my face and heard her whisper: "Not now! If you want, I'll wait for you at six, when the shop shuts."

At that moment we heard loud voices coming from the shop. They grew louder and louder. I quickly stepped forward, Daniela put the kettle down on the bench, and both of us ran into the supermarket.

There, between the shelves, stood an ugly wizened old man wearing ludicrously large, baggy trousers. In one white hand he held a metal cane, in the other a carp, his ruddy face aflame with fury. He was yelling at the top of his voice, and I gathered that he had bought a carp from us a little earlier and when he got home and weighed it had discovered that he had been cheated. By at least two crowns.

I was petrified, feeling as if I had just been caught out in some million-crown swindle.

The manager, on the other hand, was his usual calm, smiling self. He offered to weigh the fish again and exchange it for another or refund any money the old gentleman might have been overcharged, no one was infallible, but he could honestly not remember when they had last had any complaint of this nature. But the old man would not part with the *corpus delicti,* perhaps he was not even interested in getting his money back but just wanted to yell at us and make a scene. The manager—and I was amazed to find how much I admired his cool—took the old gent by the elbow and propelled him delicately past the check-outs and out of the shop, soft-soaping him all the time as he did so. He asked him to keep calm, urged him to take into account his, the manager's unblemished reputation, and again suggested that the customer have the carp reweighed, either here or elsewhere if he did not trust us.

"You're damned right, I don't trust you!" shouted the old man. "And I *will* get it weighed somewhere else." And with this he shuffled off.

Daniela's yellow head leaned closer to me and I again felt her breath as she explained that the crusty old man was Mr Vondráček, who weighed everything he brought home on his scales, even the content of tins, and then returned to raise hell in the shop. All the staff knew him and would usually give him more than he was entitled to but he never came back to *return* anything. Now of course he would go and have the carp weighed, but I wasn't to worry, the only scale he trusted anywhere in the vicinity was at the butcher's, and Mr. Koňas, the butcher, would take care of it. Winking at me, she said that Mr. Koňas had little magnetic bits of metal which, if need be, he would attach to the bottom of his scales where they could not be seen. When he took the meat off the scales he would unobtrusively remove the bits of metal so that the customer was no wiser and thought he was getting the proper weight.

Less than an hour later—I was by this time again out in the cold, weighing and wrapping up the carp we had resuscitated so that they could be murdered for profit—a broad-shouldered, red-cheeked man in a white apron turned up, and I was sure this had to be Mr. Koňas the butcher. As he approached, Mr. Koňas informed us at the top of his voice that we owed him a hefty carp. "You see lads," he exclaimed joyfully, "I weighed the fish for the old duffer and told him that you *had* made a mistake of twenty pence in the price—but in his favor! *And* I explained that a fish isn't a lump of cheese, that it loses weight fast as the water drains away from inside. He gaped at me just like a fish, his mouth wide open, and I bet you he won't bother you again for a month at least."

The butcher was still speaking when the manager hauled a plump, two-kilo carp out of the tank, killed it with a blow to the head with a heavy screwdriver, wrapped it up and handed it to Mr. Koňas. And just then it came to me that in this world of ours there existed real conspirators, that there was a far-reaching conspiracy of those who had seen through the futility of all ideals and the deadly ambiguity of all human illusions, a resolute brotherhood of true materialists who knew that the only things that mattered were those you could hold in your hand or put in your pocket, that money could buy anything and that anyone could be bribed—except Death, which they preferred to ignore, and a few foolish individuals who could be locked up in prison, exiled out of the country or at the very least into subterranean boiler rooms, there to stoke furnaces and think their wayward thoughts. While I on the whole was one of the fools, at this moment I happened to be with the others, having been invited into their midst. Yes, now both Peter and I were one of *them,* enjoying their protection and solidarity. God help me, I almost wallowed in the warm feeling which comes of *belonging.* We carried on selling carp all that afternoon. More and more customers showed up, most of them women, until they formed a long line. The weather had turned a little warmer, and there was a touch of spring in the faint breeze. How much more pleasant it would have been out in the country, taking a long walk among the meadows—for me as well as for all these people waiting their turn in the line. But they had decided that they must have a carp, on top of the mountain of pork and beef and smoked meats, the potato salad, apple strudel, brawn and ice cream and bowls full of Christmas sweetmeats they had baked these past few days.

I realized that I was beginning to hate this multitude, to despise all these people, and that this was the first part of my initiation into the general conspiracy.

Fortunately, at a quarter past five we did away with our last victim. Then we had to clean the tank, put the wooden counter back in the storeroom, return the miraculous scales with our thanks, and count our takings. Peter took charge of the money while I went out again to sweep the pavement. And, since there was less litter than cash, I finished first. Going back to the storeroom, where that morning Daniela and I had cut up the dead carp, I sat down on a chair and closed my eyes. The air was warm and moist, the place was filled with assorted aromas, and hot water bubbled in the kettle. I reflected for a while longer about the general conspiracy. Not that I thought of it as some kind of Mafia; none, or at least certainly not the majority, of its members had any criminal intent, nor were they intentionally dishonest. They were, rather, ordinary, average people who had not been offered a single idea, a single worthwhile goal that would have given meaning to their life, and they themselves had not found the strength of character to discover them on their own. This is how a whole community of the defeated had come into being, bringing together a motley crew of butchers, greengrocers, Party secretaries and factory managers, bribed supervisors and coalmen and corrupt newpapermen and, no doubt, also those who had been appointed to uncover and smash this conspiracy.

My reverie was interrupted by the sound of soft footsteps, and looking up I saw the yellow-haired Miss Daniela, now without her white coat and dressed only in a blue skirt and white blouse. "Mr. Ivan," she whispered, "do you still want to...?" And she beckoned me to follow her, leading the way to the opposite corner where the big crate stood behind all those shelves. Seeing it at close quarters I noticed that it had handles on each side, like a cabin trunk. "Here," whispered Daniela, lifting the lid of the mammoth coffin. Inside, I could see, everything was ready: blankets and two pillows.

Daniela quickly unbuttoned her blouse, while I made a start by hurriedly shedding my boots. Then we both squeezed into the crate. As I was lowering myself down next to her I saw that there was yet another handle on the inside of the lid, and I raised myself up again to pull it shut over us.

It was now almost completely dark inside the crate, just a gleam of light seeming to come from her yellow hair. Perhaps it was the peroxide—how should I know?

"Darling," I said emitting the customary sigh, and embraced her half-naked body.

"Be quiet, Mr. Ivan," she whispered. "You have to be quiet as a mouse, they'll be here in a minute." I felt her pushing my palms away from her body, then her flipper slipping inside my trousers.

"Mr. Ivan," she whispered hotly. "I saw straightaway you weren't just any old student come to earn a little pocket money before Christmas, and I didn't believe you'd been inside, neither. Your friend told me what you do, that you write plays for TV and earn heaps of money. Oh, Mr. Ivan," she was by now agitating my penis with both hands, "what's twenty thousand to you. I've saved up the rest and I know about a service station where we'd get it back in six months and anything we earned after that would be ours to keep."

"You mean you want me to come in with you?" I asked, astonished.

"I'll marry you and I'll be faithful to you for the rest of my life," whispered Miss Daniela passionately. "That station is right by the highway, all the truck drivers use it and lots of those that go abroad, too. In a couple of years we'll make enough to buy a house, and you can have a brand new car and we'll go on holiday to the seaside. We'll have a marvelous life, what do you say?"

I heard someone calling my name outside, and, still bemused by Miss Daniela's loving touch, I quickly threw the lid open. Jumping onto the concrete floor, I ran outside to join Peter in my bare feet—or rather in my three pairs of woolen socks.

"I just don't understand how this could've happened," Peter said, standing there with several bundles of banknotes in his hand. He was so shocked that he failed to notice the disordered state of my attire.

"What's wrong?"

"That scale was fixed," Peter lamented, "and we sold twenty carp in portions for almost twice their proper price, *and* you charged the customers the way the manager showed us."

"Well, I did the best I could," I said, suddenly feeling that I had to stand up for myself. "Did we make a loss?"

He nodded but did not reply.

"How much?"

"Eight hundred."

"You mean we've lost what we put in?"

He shook his head. "No, over and above that." He looked as

if he were about to burst into tears.

"Oh, to hell with it," I said. "To hell with all the money."

The savings banks would still be open tomorrow morning. I would take out two thousand and take it to the wife of my colleague who was locked up because he refused to join the great conspiracy.

"I just can't understand how it could've happened," said Peter plaintively. "All those fish, and we must've made at least two crowns on each one of them."

I shrugged. In my mind's eye I could see all those conspirators, stealthily advancing on our fish tank under cover of the frosty night: our manager leading the way, followed by Mr. Koňas the butcher and the yellow-haired Daniela and all the greengrocers and Party secretaries, factory managers and bribed supervisors, coal merchants and corrupt newspapermen...Each and every one of them thrusting greedy hands into our tank and scuttling away with our carp...

"All I can say is that next time you want to sell carp you'd better spend the night with them."

"You think so?" His eyes seemed to light up as he got the message, but all he did was shrug his shoulders.

Well, I guess he was right, at that. It would have been no use. *They* would always find a way to cheat us, we just didn't belong.

In 1960, Ivan Klíma's first short story collection was published in his native land. He is also an essayist, novelist and playwright. In 1970, he had been banned from publishing in Czechoslovakia. Today, under President Havel, Ivan Klíma can again openly be published in Czechoslovakia. His writings are widely translated into German. He had been a visiting professor at the University of Michigan in 1969-1970; but in the spring of 1970, Czechs abroad were refused extensions of their exit permits and he returned to Prague. George Theiner, his translator, is a Czech-born editor and journalist who left Czechoslovakia in 1968. He is presently the editor of Index on Censorship.

"His one burning ambition was to sight his six thousandth bird."

The Six Thousandth Bird

BY NIGEL WATT

DAVID Sedgewick delicately touched the fine focusing knob on his *spotter* scope, and the cream and brown distinctive markings of the Barred Owl, perched in a bare tree on the far side of the river, sprang into sharp view.

He smiled faintly with a quiet sense of inner satisfaction. It wasn't a rare bird—he had probably seen more than two dozen of them during his thirty-five years of bird-watching—but his experience had told him precisely where to look and his sharp eyes had spotted it at a great distance before he set up the telescope on his tripod to examine it more closely.

It certainly was beautiful and it sat motionless with all the nobility of a fierce predator, but well camouflaged by the contours of the tree. The muddy flow of the Mekong River and gravelly foreshore separated David from his quarry. Quietly, with time-practiced precision David extracted a travel-stained notebook from his pocket and made an entry of his sighting with a black ballpoint pen; had the bird been of a species David had never seen before he would have entered it in his notebook in red ink. Then it would be, as he and his *birder* colleagues called it, a life-tick, to add to the ever growing variety of bird species he had personally identified in his international travels. His list of the number of bird species spotted since his boyhood now totaled an amazing 5,998, nearly half the entire catalog of recorded varieties throughout the world. Adding to this list was a passion which amounted to an addiction which ruled his life.

It all had started when his father gave him a pair of binoculars for his thirteenth birthday. Suddenly those boring after-lunch Sunday walks with his family through the Gloucestershire woods near his childhood home were transformed into exciting adventures as the wonders of nature were revealed to him.

He took a zoology degree at Bristol University and followed that with an eminent doctorate in ornithology. Then his travels and his life as a conservationist began. Forest surveys in Europe and South America, bird surveys in Central America, Indonesia and Malaysia, panda protection studies in China and computer systems for nature research in Thailand. The inevitable administrative duties of these various projects were a distraction from his bird-watching but his every spare moment was devoted to this passion and the traveling helped him to add to his list of *life-ticks*.

Now, at forty-eight years of age, he had sixty-seven carefully annotated notebooks of the tens of thousands of birds he had seen, including the 5,998 individual varieties. But his collector's addiction had cost him a high price. His wife had left him after only three years of marriage. He had no family ties and his life was that of a wandering gypsy living roughly wherever the birds took him. His one burning ambition was to sight his six thousandth bird; then, he said to himself, without really believing it, "I will stop."

Here on the Mekong River, in Xishuangbanna Autonomous Prefecture in Southern China, close to the Laos and Myanmar borders, he hoped to achieve this ambition. But it was no longer easy to add to his long list of sightings and it might take weeks to find only one more new species, although he would see dozens of birds that he had seen before. He was with a party of six other eminent *birders* who had been assembled to undertake a forest survey for China which would help in the planning of future nature reserves, not only in China but elsewhere.

The country was rough, and living for the team was simple, sometimes bedding down under mosquito nets in the comparative luxury of forestry stations, or, on other occasions, after a day fighting off leeches in the dripping foliage of the rain forest, stretching out on the communal slatted wooden floor of a Dai or Bulang village hut.

At this moment the entourage was on its way into the mountains to survey forest at higher altitudes but had been temporarily frustrated in their journey by a broken bridge across a Mekong tributary which had cut the road. While the drivers were discussing whether the four-wheel drive Land Rovers could negotiate a muddy ravine higher up the stream, the *birders* were seizing the enforced stop to add to their bird lists. Like David Sedgewick they were all driven on by the same compulsion. Not a moment to waste as they separated along their chosen paths in a high state of competition, with binoculars and notebooks at the ready. In the evening, by the light of candles, they would exchange their notes, share a beer and argue about the identifiable features of the birds they had seen. But today was only a short break en route and soon the drivers would be calling them back to the cars.

David was now studying the lanky shape of a Thick-Knees in the mud flats of the river as the motor horns sounded. He completed his notes, shouldered his tripod, and made his way back to the car, joining other members of the team on the way. They clambered over stepping stones across the slippery ravine to join the cars which had crossed successfully and were waiting for their passengers on the other side.

Despite the broken bridge, the earth-surfaced road up into

the mountains was in surprisingly good shape, and the survey team in their two vehicles made good time. Their aim was to get to their base village by 4:00 p.m., in time to do some birding before sunset and the evening meal. Then, the next day, there would be a walk of about twelve miles to the isolated forest village where the main survey would take place.

The drive took them past stretches of rice paddies, fields of vegetables, and remote village factories which had stripped the local forest to provide fuel for the drying of tea and tobacco. As the road climbed higher the trees lining the road became more extensive. Throughout the journey the *birders* were all looking keenly into the depths of the passing trees and listening acutely for any bird calls. While passing through one of these forested areas, David suddenly capped a hand to his ear and with the other touched the driver on the shoulder. "Stop, please, quickly," he said.

Startled, the driver rammed on his brakes and the Land Rover jolted to a sudden stop, throwing the passengers roughly forward. "Hey, what the hell are you doing, David?" someone shouted.

"Sorry," muttered David as he leapt from the Land Rover and disappeared into the canopy of trees lining the road.

It was a full fifteen minutes before he reappeared smiling broadly. His stocky figure seemed to walk with a new vigor and his blue eyes shone even more brightly than usual.

"Feeling better?" taunted one of his colleagues. "What's wrong old boy—taken short or something?"

David responded by waving his notebook jubilantly "I thought I heard it, and I did—because I found it in the trees," he said excitedly. "A beautiful Great Barbet. Not a particularly rare bird, but the first time I've seen one. So its a *life-tick* for me, and it's my five thousandth, nine hundred and ninety-ninth bird. I only want one more to achieve my ambitlon—six thousand different bird species. The beer's on me tonight, boys."

There were handshakes and back-slapping all round as they joined in David's jubilation and quickly overcame their frustration at having been left stranded at the roadside for a quarter of an hour.

The enthusiasm was infectious and when they reached the village, dusty and tired, most of the party grabbed their binoculars and telescopes and, without waiting for beers to slake their thirst were off to see if they could match David's good fortune.

The village headman welcomed the team leader and invited him into his house to discuss the evening meal, the sleeping arrangements and the hire of porters, who would be needed for the next day's mountain hike.

His house was typical of the other eight huts in the village clearing. A steeply gabled thatched roof towered above a great square, slatted timber floor raised some eight feet on stout wooden piles. Under the floor, which was reached by a heavy wooden-pegged staircase, were the chickens, pigs and farm implements. Water buffalo were returning from the adjoining fields and were also stabled there for the night. The great floor, about forty feet square, had a thick, clay slab in the center on which an open fire burnt ready for the cooking of the evening meal. The smoke rose up into the recesses of the roof which was blackened with heavy, sticky tar, the result of years of cooking. Candles and primilive oil lamps hanging near the fire provided the lighting. The walls of the upper room were boarded or covered with rush mats. The main food preparation took place on a small, open "verandah" made of strips of split bamboo, which was also set on poles and projected from one side of the square floor.

On this open platform the headman's wife was busy preparing a meal for the influx of visitors. Steamed rice, forest mushrooms and boiled chicken, accompanied by a special welcoming soup made from the blood of a freshly killed cockerel, were on the menu.

Before dark, the birding party returned full of news of their latest sightings. They exchanged notes with one another as they washed in the small stream adjoining the headman's patch of banana trees. Then they joined him and their expedition leader on the upper floor of the hut for the evening meal.

Talk centered on birds in the area and their habitat. "Is the rare Peacock Pheasant still seen in the area?" David asked through the team's interpreter.

"Yes," replied the headman. "But it's a shy bird, easily distracted by noise and very hard to find. However, you may be lucky tomorrow. You're going to the right area."

"Wonderful," said David excitedly. "The very bird I need."

"But be careful," warned the headman. "Tomorrow's route is precipitous and slippery. Stick to the paths."

Early the next morning they set out on the mountain trail. Much of their heavier equipment and supplies they left with the cars at the village. But there was still enough to load up a couple of hardy mountain porters, who set off ahead of the main group.

It was a beautiful trail but exhausting for the hikers. It meandered inexorably upwards, occasionally fooling the travelers by rounding a corner and decending only to find it wasn't the top but simply a lesser ridge on the way to the forested summit.

It wandered down little ravines and across streams bridged by single tree trunks across which the *birders* gingerly threaded their way. In the lower reaches, it circled patches of rice paddies and passed through little Balang villages where the villagers, in bright, colorful clothes, wended their way to and from their fields accompanied by the inevitable water buffalo. In places it was steep and slippery, and little waterfalls trickled down the hillsides.

It was in one such place the party stopped to rest for a few minutes. They scattered themselves around.

David stretched out on a leafy bank, his hands behind his head, glad to have a chance to recover from the exertions of the climb. As he looked through the lacery of the foliage above and at the blue sky with its occasional flecks of passing fleecy clouds, he felt strangely contented with his lot. This was precisely what he asked of life and he had no real regrets—except that missing bird.

Then he heard it. Almost imperceptibly at first but, like his eyesight, David's hearing was incredibly sharp. Then the faint sound came again from the depths of the forest slopes beneath him. He was sure it was the cry of the Peacock Pheasant. Nobody else had heard it. They were all resting quietly.

Quickly, David got to his feet and cautiously groped his way into the forest slopes below the path. Moving quietly, he heard the sound again, this time a little nearer. His heart was beating faster and his breathing was a little quicker. Whether this was due to his excitement or exertion was of little matter.

He had one aim: to find that bird. No other thought entered his head. He had totally forgotten his colleagues and the warnings of the headman. The vision of the Peacock Pheasant filled his mind, his hopes, his imagination, to the exclusion of all else.

By now he had descended some hundred feet below the path. The foliage was wet and treacherous. He held on to saplings to lower himself as quietiy as he could.

Then, there it was again, quite close this time, maybe thirty or forty feet beneath him. He eagerly grasped another young sapling. But as he began to lower himself to the next muddy level of the forest floor, it snapped apart and his heavy body slid out of control over and over to a ravine at least forty feet beneath.

"Damn!" he muttered to himself, and then unconsciousness overtook him as his head cracked against a passing tree stump.

When he came to he was conscious of lying on his back, incapable of movement, with a total numbness in the lower part of his body. He could hear the noise of running water from a nearby stream. He could still see above his head the tracery of branches and foliage framing the sky.

All was quiet and still.

Then he heard it again. So close this time his heart almost missed a beat. The Peacock Pheasant of Xishwuangbanna. He managed by extreme effort, and despite the pain, to ease his head a little to the right. And there it was in all its glory in the clearing only twenty feet away from him. He scarcely dared to breathe. Joy welled up in him. A life-tick! His six thousandth bird! How long he watched he didn't know—it could have been two minutes or twenty. For David it was pure ecstasy. A smile flecked the corners of his mouth and the pain of his injuries seemed to disappear.

Then, having given David this private display, the pheasant moved out of the clearing and disappeared into the thick undergrowth.

David, with effort, managed slowly to move his right arm and drag with his fingertips from his breast-pocket his precious notebook with the dual-colored ballpoint pen attached. He laid the book on his chest, opened it at the marker where he knew there was a predated blank page on the right-hand side and awkwardly scrawled in red ink:

6000 - PEACOCK PHEASANT

Then, securing the book firmly against his stomach with his arm, he closed his eyes, exhausted. But he was a serenely, happy man.

When the search party found him they would have no doubt about that!

Nigel Watt, born in 1922, is a journalist and photographer by training who has turned to short story writing. He has worked in Central Africa, South Arabia and the Far East in public relations and broadcasting, and recently retired as Commissioner for Television and Entertainment Licensing in Hong Kong. His articles and photo-features have appeared in newspapers and periodicals throughout the world.

"The orange smacked the center of his chest
with a shocking thud..."

The Orange

BY JEROME MANDEL

"I'M going out for my walk, honey. Want to come?"

She looked up from her book. Standing in the middle of
the living room in cut-off jeans and a stained T-shirt, her
husband looked more like a kid or a refugee than the forty-four
year old president of an electronics company recently sold for
two-and-a-half million in cash plus four million in stock, a
willing victim in what had become known as the battle of the
mini-conglomerates. Early in life he had won at the game of
making money, and now he didn't have to play anymore. He
was through with the boardroom and the factory. He had left
the battlefield behind them in Chicago and come to live in this
northern suburb of Tel Aviv. And since he had all the money
he needed to do whatever he wanted, he could afford to dress
in rags.

"I'm not sure I want to be seen in public with you in that
outfit."

"What are you talking about? These are my most disreputable clothes."

He raised his arms as if in surrender and turned slowly so she could see how faded and threadbare his clothes were. Since coming to Israel and earnestly committing himself to walking, he had lost about eighteen pounds.

"Oh beautiful, really beautiful," she said.

"Thank you, madame. But enough admiration—are you coming or not?"

"Is this going to be a business trip?"

"What?"

"Are you walking for exercise or pleasure?"

"My exercise is my pleasure."

"Ah-ha!" she said. "There you go again. Reconciling opposites. It may have worked for labor and management, but when you walk for exercise, I need the car to keep up with you."

"And if I walk for your pleasure, I've got to stand in front of every shop window in town."

"And never raise a sweat."

"How can I raise a sweat if I'm standing in front of a shop window?"

"I'll tell you what, my dear. You go out and sweat as much as you like, and I'll sit here with my book, and when you come back and take a shower and put on some nice clothes and your Guccis, we can go out to dinner. We're invited to the Wellmans' at 9:30. Go out and play in the traffic now, and don't bother me anymore. And don't get killed."

With an impish salute, he turned smartly on his heels, but just as he reached the door, the buzzer sounded.

He opened the door with a smile and looked into the empty hall.

"It's the intercom," she said.

"Hello," he said brightly into the phone that connected his apartment with the front security door. "Hello?" No one answered.

"Must be the children playing with the intercom again."

"Bye, dear."

"Bye."

Gilbert Martin stepped briskly out of the cool darkness beneath his building into the blinding afternoon. The westering sun was past its great heat. The air was still and solemn with the clarity of thick crystal, presupposing languor and siesta. No dogs barked. No cars moved. Even the children had not yet come out from the shaded parking areas under the buildings to play in the afternoon sun and among the lengthening shadows.

He turned away from the little town toward the orange groves at the far end of his street. The road he wanted to walk skirted the orchards, turned sandy and climbed the hill near the cemetery, became asphalt again and ran west toward the sea. To the right lay the villas and apartment houses of the town, uniformly white in the dust. To the left, beyond an ancient house or two, lay the green fields and orchards of a pretty *moshav* that would eventually be swallowed up by expanding Tel Aviv.

The trees were already beginning to take on their coats of white summer dust, and the raw new buildings of the town, softening with young wisteria and ivy, had begun to sprout windowboxes of pink geraniums and lush succulents.

When he came to the orange grove, he walked quickly on the sunny side of the road, away from the trees. He peered down the long ranks and into the shadows beneath the trees, but found no terrorists lurking there. He didn't really expect to—he lived too far from the interface with violence—but he had read enough stories to know where the terrorists liked to lurk. He did, however, start a hare with immense ears who must have thought he was a predator and darted away among the orderly rows of trees.

He maintained the same brisk pace as he walked up the hill to the cemetery. He started to sweat. Coming down the other side along the fringes of the town, he saw a skinny kid wobbling on a bike too big for him. His sister ran beside him and tried to help him keep his balance by holding onto the handlebars, but her position was awkward; she turned the wheel and he tumbled into the dust beside the road. He skipped away without a bruise, but he took a fistful of roadside sand and stone and hurled it in a white cloud at his fleeing sister.

High above a bell-pepper field a hawk hung motionless against the light. It seemed painted there, permanent. And then, without a wrinkle, it slipped down the sky in a gentle arc and hung again farther off.

As Gilbert came to the end of the street that marked the margin between the town and the fields, he turned down a narrow road that led back through an area of large private houses toward the center of town. Two puppies, still in their first fur, their coats seemingly too large for them, tumbled in the dust, playing with their teeth at each other's throats. A man with sharp shears looked up from pruning shrubs to watch him pass.

He swung down the narrow road, happy in the day, happy to be idle and active. He looked at all the expensive villas with their grass and gardens, secretly pleased not to be concerned with such things. His penthouse roof-garden was just enough to be amusing without being work. What a lovely day!

A white Volkswagen turned from the town onto the road ahead of him. It was coming fast. He stepped off the road onto the sandy margin and looked up in time to see the most amazing sight. An orange was miraculously, wonderfully, suspended between him and the oncoming car. It hung in the air by magic. It was beautiful, improbable, the only surprising dash of color on the white road, superimposed upon the white car between the white houses. He watched with amazement and delight.

The car screamed past with a rush of mechanical noise. The orange smacked the center of his chest with a shocking thud and, breathless and dazed, he dropped to his knees in the sand, bewildered. Stone cut into his flesh as he sat over on one leg, half-on, half-off the road. The orange lay motionless beside him. It was gashed open, the bright innards bleeding.

"Damn it!" he said, as he stood up suddenly, scattering stone and sand in a cloud of white dust. He peered down the road, but the car was gone. He strode off purposefully in the direction he had come, looking for the white Volkswagen. He was going to kill the people inside.

At the end of the street where the puppies were still tumbling over each other, he saw several cars parked in front of a high house. One was a white Volkswagen, but it was facing in the wrong direction, down the narrow road he had just come up. He put his hand on the rear bonnet to see if he could feel the heat of the engine. The bonnet was warm, but the late afternoon sun was full upon it. The other cars were equally warm, or almost so. He went up to the man with the shears who was still worrying over his shrubs.

"Excuse me," said Gilbert in Hebrew.

"Speak also English," said the man, trying to be helpful.

"Well, then," said Gilbert, relieved, "you may remember that I just walked down this road here, maybe five minutes ago."

The man nodded either because he understood what Gilbert said or because he confirmed that what Gilbert said was true.

"Between then and now, did this Volkswagen come up this road?"

The man continued to nod.

"Then why is it facing the opposite direction? Ah! I get it. The car came up this way and turned around so to be facing the way it had come. Very clever. Do you have a telephone?"

"Telephone? Yes." He led the way into his house.

"I want to call the police," said Gilbert.

"The police?" The man suddenly looked sober. He put down his pruning shears.

"You didn't happen to see who got out of the car, did you?"

"What?"

"Who was driving the car?"

"No. None."

Gilbert spoke to the police, turning once to ask the man, "What's the address here?"

"Sixty-four Yehuda HaNassi," said the thoughtful man.

"Sixty-four Yehuda HaNassi. That's right. I'll be standing out in front. Gilbert Martin."

When the blue police van pulled up in front of the house, two men and two women got out, dressed in the pressed khaki uniform of the Israeli police.

"Would you tell us exactly what happened, Mr. Gilbert?"

one of the policewomen asked.

As Gilbert explained, the taller, darker policeman was translating for the other two.

"And this is the car, I'm sure of it," said Gilbert. "This man saw it pull up. And it turned around, you see, so that it would look as though it had come from the other direction."

"Well, let's go talk to the owner."

"Just a minute," said the tall policeman. "You said you are sure this is the same car."

"Yes."

"How are you sure?"

"Well, it's the only Volkswagen here."

"There are many white Volkswagens in Israel. Did you see the registration?"

"The what?"

"The registration. The number."

"Oh, you mean the license plate. No. It was too fast."

"Did you see any special marks on the car?"

"No."

"And you say the car came up this narrow road."

"That's right."

"It's in the wrong direction."

"I told you. It turned around."

"But you did not see it turn around."

"No. But this man did." Gilbert indicated the man whose phone he had used. "He's a witness."

"Okay. We shall see. Now let's talk to Mussa."

"Who's Mussa?"

"He lives here. He owns the car."

"You know him?"

"Yes. He is well known."

"Mussa. Is that a Jewish name?" asked Gilbert.

"Mussa comes from Baghdad. His name is Arabic for Moses. He is like you a Jew. But a dark one. Like me. Eastern Jew. Sephardi. You understand me?"

Gilbert understood only that the distance between Iraq and Illinois was not easily reconciled.

As they went through the gate and up to the imposing house, one of the policewomen stayed behind to talk to the witness. Gilbert could see the man shake his head, lift his shoulders, and spread his arms in the Mediterranean gesture of individual bafflement before implacable and completely unreasonable reality.

The door was opened by a handsome man in his mid-sixties with a sun-crinkled face, thick black hair with a touch of white at the temples, and a white moustache drooped and shaped as Gilbert had seen among the Druse elders. Even dressed in dusty, sun-bleached clothes, the man exuded energy and power. He welcomed the police into a small foyer where they all started talking rapidly in Hebrew.

Gilbert couldn't follow and wasn't really interested. He was looking beyond the discussion and into the house. A young man draped in gold chains sat on a white sofa with another young man and drank from a full glass of beer. They ignored the police completely, secure, Gilbert realized, in Mussa's ability to protect them.

"What's he saying?" Gilbert asked the policewoman who had spoken English to him. But she held up her thumb and two fingers pressed together as if she were balancing a marble. Gilbert knew enough Hebrew to know the gesture meant "just a moment." Then the policewoman who had been interrogating Gilbert's witness came in and started talking rapidly to the tall policeman who seemed to be in charge.

"What's going on? What's he saying?"

"He says there has been some mistake," said the policewoman.

"What mistake?"

"Mussa says his wife was driving the car. She was in the supermarket. The vegetables are here in the kitchen. Mussa says she came home a little time ago but she did not come up this narrow road. She came up the big road next to the fields. That's why the car is parked facing down the narrow road. Mussa says his sons have been here for an hour with him. Mussa says many cars come down the narrow road and drive away. The people come from somewhere else. They don't belong here. And there are many Volkswagens in Israel."

"But what about the man next door? That's not what he says."

"Ah, yes. This man thinks you maybe did not understand. He saw nothing."

"Nothing?"

The tall policeman was thanking Mussa and backing everyone out of the house as the two insouciant boys continued to neglect them.

"God damn it!" said Gilbert when they were all standing out on the road in the early evening. "Those boys did it. I know they did it. I don't care what anybody says."

"Yes. Of course," said the tall policeman. "Mussa protects them."

"But if you know they did it, why don't you arrest them? I want to file a complaint."

"I have no facts. No evidence."

"What about the man next door? Can't you make him tell the truth?"

"He lives here. He is Mussa's neighbor. He must protect himself and his family."

"Damn it," said Gilbert. "I'm going to press charges anyway. Let's settle the matter in court."

"You can do this if you like to. But you must talk to a lawyer first. Discuss the facts with him. Then if you want to make a complaint, come to the police station."

Gilbert had been in enough negotiations to know when he was being finessed. "What's your name?" he asked.

"Avi."

"Avi, you said that you knew Mussa, that he was known to the police."

"Yes."

"What for?"

"Mussa does prostitution."

"Prostitution?"

"Yes. We will get him and his sons maybe one day. But not today."

"Prostitution? What kind of a job is that for a Jew?"

Avi looked at him with amusement.

"The girls are Jewish, too," he said.

"What!"

"Yes. It is a vicious business. And Mussa is a violent man. I do not want anyone hurt on such a small business of an orange. Talk to your lawyer. Tell him everything. But if you listen to what I tell you, you will forget about this. You will not win. You have not facts."

"But I have the will to win."

Avi looked at him.

"I can be ruthless," said Gilbert, remembering his triumphs in the boardroom.

"You are an American, yes?"

"From Chicago," said Gilbert, smiling.

They stood about in awkward silence. Gilbert felt he was missing something.

"What's going on?" he said.

"Can I give you a tramp back to your house?"

"No, thank you. I'm walking for my health."

"Talk to your lawyer first," said Avi, getting into the police van beside the others. "Then if you want to make a complaint..."

"Yes."

Gilbert walked home through the evening the way he had come—among the fields and houses, past the cemetery and the orchards.

He opened the security door with his key and rang for the elevator. He turned, by chance, to look out into the street, and, just before the door closed, he glimpsed a white Volkswagen. As the security door clicked shut before him, the elevator doors opened behind him. He stepped inside quickly.

"Hello, dear. Did you have a nice walk? You've been gone a long time."

"No, I did not. I've been with the police."

"What happened? What did you do?"

"I didn't do anything. I was attacked."

"Attacked?"

"Some kids threw an orange at me out of a fast-moving car."

"Assault with a deadly orange, eh?"

"It's not funny, Loretta."

"I'm sorry, dear, but you seem to be fine. Did it hit you?"

"Hit me! It damn near killed me. Bowled me over. There I was, groveling in the dust, trying to catch my breath."

"But you're not hurt."

"No."

"Well, no harm done. Thank God for that."

"But I know who did it and that's why I called the police."

"Did the police arrest them?"

"No. Not enough evidence, they say. Not enough hard facts."

"Then it's over. The Attack of the Flying Orange People! Disreputable Victim Disheveled! Perpetrators Unpunished. Call in Poirot!"

"It's not funny and it's not over."

"What do you mean it's not over? Are you going to press charges anyway?"

"Maybe. I want to talk to Wellman tonight and see what he says. It seems that the people who did this are part of a criminal family, into drugs and prostitution, and, you know, they're not Arabs. They're Jews."

"Criminals?"

"Yes. The police told me all about them."

"Jewish criminals? Here in Israel?"

"This certainly isn't Chicago."

She seemed to consider this.

"If you want some advice from a wife who loves you," she said, "you'll forget about it. Kids will be kids. No harm was done. Perhaps your pride got a little dusty is all—but then, you're dressed for that, aren't you?"

"I can't wear a business suit when I go for a walk," he said.

"Will you change, please, before we go out? Do you want a bite to eat here or shall we go out to dinner before we go to the Wellmans'?"

"I want to wear these clothes to the Wellmans'."

"Victim of Assault by Ferocious Orange Throws Himself upon Mercy of Court in Original Rags."

"Very funny."

"Have the Wellmans ever seen you in your original rags?"

"They're naïve," said Gilbert. "They think that people are the way they seem to be. I'm going to expose them to the dark underside of Israeli society."

"I hope at least that you're going to shower your dark underside before you go exposing it all over the place."

"I will," he said, moving off toward the bathroom.

"And change your clothes."

As Gilbert passed the door, the buzzer sounded. After an awkward moment he opened the door and looked out into the dark hallway.

"It's the intercom," she said.

He picked up the phone and listened. "Hello," he said. No one answered.

"Kids," said Loretta.

But Gilbert pulled open the sliding windows in the living room and walked across the penthouse garden to look down into the street in front of their building. Three white Volkswagens. Were there so many in the neighborhood?

As he watched, he became aware of night replacing evening, of darkness whelming up from the east and falling everywhere. He closed the windows and pulled the sheers against the darkness and, as he went past the front door on his way to the showers, he turned the key in the lock.

Jerome Mandel settled permanently in Israel in 1979. He was born in 1937, in Cleveland, Ohio, and earned his Ph.D. in 1966 from Ohio State University. He teaches on the university level and has published extensively on Old and Middle English literature, focusing primarily on Chaucer and medieval romance. His current book is the The Architectonics of the Canterbury Tales.

"Without ceremony and without the law, they were wedded by a tacitly sworn agreement between themselves."

Tanabata's Wife

BY SINAI C. HAMADA

FAS-ANG first came to Baguio by way of the Mountain Trail. When at last she emerged from her weary travel over the mountains, she found herself just above the Trinidad Valley. From there, she overlooked the city of Baguio itself.

Baguio was her destination. Along with three other women, she had planned to come to work on the numerous roads that were being built around the city. Native women were given spades to shovel the earth from the hillsides, and so make way for the roads that were being cut.

They had almost arrived. Yet Fas-ang knew of no place where she could live in the city while waiting to be taken on as a laborer. Perhaps she would stay in the workers' camp and be packed with the other laborers in their smelly quarters. She had heard a lot about the tiered beds, the congestion in the long low-roofed house for the road workers.

It was midafternoon. The four women and three men,

new immigrants from Bontoc, walked on the long straight road of the Trinidad Valley. They had never before in their lives seen a road so long and straight. After the regular up and down journey over the hills, the level road was tedious and slow to travel on.

Plodding along, they at last left the valley behind, passed through the narrow gap of the Trinidad River, and entered Lucban Valley. All along the road, the sight was a succession of cabbage plots, more and more.

When they had passed Lucban Valley and came to Kisad Valley, still there were rows and rows of cabbages. But now the sun was sinking low behind the brown hills in the west. And the company thought of their shelter for the night, for they had one more steep hill to climb before the city laborers' camp. So they had been told. Their feet ached painfully. Was there no door open for them among the thatched homes in the valley?

It was then that they came to the house of Tanabata-san. The Japanese gardener was looking out through his tiny window as they were about to pass on. He halted them.

"Are you looking for work?" the gardener called out in his broken dialect.

"Indeed we are, my lord," one of the strangers replied.

"If you like, I have work for two women, in my garden," Tanabata offered.

The men looked questioningly at the women. "Which of you would like to stay?" one man asked.

Only Fas-ang was willing to consider the gardener's offer. She stepped forward. "How much would you give me?" she demanded.

"Ten pesos."

"Ten peso?" Fas-ang asked for twelve, but Tanabata would not agree to that. Fas-ang again reflected for a moment, and then confided to her companions: "I guess I'll stay. There is but a difference of two pesos between what I'll get here and my wage if I become a road worker. Who knows? My lot here may even be better."

One of the remaining three women was also persuaded to stay after Fas-ang had made her decision. Tanabata was smiling as he watched the two make up their minds.

The rest of the company were going on their way. "So, you two shall stay," the eldest of the group said, affecting a superior air. "Well, if you think it is best for both of you, then it is all right. You need not worry over us, for we shall go on and reach the camp early tonight."

In this way, Fas-ang first lent herself to Tanabata. She was then at the height of womanhood. Her cheeks were ruddy, though not as rosy as in her girlhood. She had a buxom breast, the main charm of her sturdy self. As she walked, her footsteps were heavy. And anyone would admit that she was indeed pretty.

Tanabata had had no wife. For a long time now, he had been looking for one among the native women, hoping he would find one who might consent to marry him. But none did he ever find, until Fas-ang, guided by fate, came. He had almost sent for a Japanese wife from his homeland. He had seen her picture. But it would have cost him much.

Would Fas-ang, by chance, learn to like him and later agree to their marriage? This was only a tiny thought in the mind of Tanabata as he sat one evening looking wistfully at Fas-ang. She was washing her feet by the water ditch in front of the house. Every now and then, she lifted her skirt above her knees, and Tanabata saw her clear, bright skin, tempting skin.

After a time, Fas-ang herself would watch Tanabata. As they sat before their supper, she would cast furtive glances at him across the low, circular table. He was bearded. Sometimes, he let his beard grow for three days, and his unshaven, hairy face was ugly to look at. Only with a clean countenance, and in his blue suit did Fas-ang like him at all.

Well-dressed, Tanabata-san would walk on Sundays to the market fair. Close behind would follow one of his laborers, carrying two heavy baskets over his shoulder. The baskets overflowed with the minor produce of the garden: strawberries, celery, tomatoes, spinach, radishes, and "everlasting" flowers. Fas-ang, in her gayest Sunday dress, would trail in the rear. She was to sell garden products at the market.

In the afternoon, the fair would be over. Fas-ang would go home with a heavy handbag. She would arrive to find Tanabata, usually tipsy, with a half-emptied bottle still before him on the table.

Fas-ang would lay the bag of money on his crossed legs. "That is the amount the vegetables have brought us," she would report.

"Good." And Tanabata would break into a happy smile. He always said gracias after that, showing full trust in Fas-ang. He would pick out two half-peso pieces and give them to her. "Here, take these. They are for you. Buy yourself whatever you like with them." He was a prosperous, generous gardener.

On weekdays, there was hard and honest work in the gardens. The other native woman had gone away when she saw that she was not so favored as Fas-ang. So, Fas-ang, when she was not cooking, stayed among the cabbage rows picking worms. All that Tanabata did was to care for the seedlings in the shed house. Also, he did most of the transplanting, since he alone had the sensitive fingers that could feel the animate sense of the soil. He had but a little area to superintend, and only three farmhands to look after.

New life! Fas-ang liked the daily turns that were her lot. Little by little she learned to do the domestic chores. Early in the morning she rose to cook. Before noon she cooked again. And in the evening likewise. She washed clothes occasionally, and more often when the laundress came irregularly. She swept the house. And, of course, she never forgot to leave a teakettle steaming over live embers. At anytime, Tanabata might come in and sip a cup of tea.

Immediately after noon on weekdays, when the sun was hot and the leaves were almost wilting, Tanabata liked to stroll and visit his neighbor, Okamoto-san. They were from the same province in Japan, Hiroshimaken. Okamoto had a

Benguet woman for a wife. Kawane was an industrious and amiable companion. The only fault Okamoto found in Kawane was her ignorance. She had no idea of the world beyond her small valley.

One afternoon, Tanabata as usual paid his friend a visit. This was of great consequence, for he had in mind to ask Okamoto if he thought Fas-ang could be a fit wife for him. Tanabata was slow in broaching the subject to his friend, but he was direct:

"I think I shall marry that woman," Tanabata said.

"Which woman—Fas-ang?" Okamoto asked.

"Yes."

"She is a good woman, I think. She seems to behave well."

"I have known her for only a short time. Do you think she will behave as well always?" Tanabata asked earnestly.

Okamoto was hesitant and would not be explicit. "I cannot tell. But look at my wife. She's a peaceful woman," he answered simply.

"There, my good friend," Tanabata reminded his neighbor, "you forget that your wife is of the Benguet tribe, while Fas-ang is of the Bontoc tribe."

"Yet they are good friends—as much as we are," was Okamoto's bright rejoinder. And they both laughed.

Two days later Tanabata proposed to Fas-ang. He had frequently teased her before. But now he was gravely concerned about what he had to tell. He had great respect for this sturdy native woman.

He called Fas-ang into the big room where she had heretofore seldom entered except to clean. It was dimly lighted. Fas-ang went in, unafraid. It seemed she had anticipated this. She sat close beside him on a trunk. Tanabata talked carefully, convincingly, and long. He explained to her as best he could, his intentions. At last, she yielded. Without ceremony and without the law, they were wedded by a tacitly sworn agreement between themselves.

As before, Fas-ang did not find it difficult to tend the truck garden. To be sure, it was sometimes dull. Now and then she would get exasperated with the routine work. But only for a short time. Ordinarily, she was patient, bending over the plants as she rid them of their worms, or gathered them for the sale in the market. Her hands had been trained now to handle with care the tender seedlings, which had to be prodded to grow luxuriantly.

When the sunbeams filled the valley, and the dewy leaves were glistening, it was a joy to watch the fluttering white butterflies that flitted all over the gardens. They were pests, for their chrysalides mercilessly devoured the green vegetables. Still, their coming in the bright morning would stir the laborers to be up and doing before they, themselves, were outdone by the insects.

In time, Fas-ang was introduced to Japanese customs. Thus she learned to use chopsticks after being prevailed upon by Tanabata; they had a zinc tub outside their hut in which they heated water and took a bath in the evening; Fas-ang pickled radishes after the Japanese fashion, salting them in a barrel; she began to use wooden shoes, though of the Filipino variety, and left them outside their bedroom before she retired; she became used to drinking tea and pouring much *toyo* sauce on their food; mattresses too, and no longer a plain mat, formed her bedding.

A year after they were married they had a child, a boy. The baby was a darling. Tanabata decided to celebrate the coming of this new being. He gave a baptismal party to which were invited his Japanese friends. They drank *saki*, ate Japanese seaweeds, pickles, canned fish, and many other dainties.

But Fas-ang, in all this revelry, could not understand the chattering of her guests. She was very quiet, holding the baby in her arms.

The men (there were no women visitors) had brought gifts for the baby and the mother. Fas-ang was very much delighted. She repeatedly muttered her *gracias* to all as the gifts were piled before her.

Then the men consulted the Japanese calendar. The child was given the name Kato. And the guests shouted *banzai* many times, tossing glassfuls of *saki* to the ceiling. They wished the mother and child good luck.

Tanabata was most solicitous toward Fas-ang as she began to recover from the emaciation caused by her strenuous childbirth. He would not allow her to go out. She must stay indoors for a month. It was another Japanese custom.

At length, when August had passed, Fas-ang once more stepped out into the sunshine, warm and free. The pallor of her cheeks had gone. She was alive and young again. Her usual springy steps came back and she walked briskly, full of strength and passion.

But what news of home? Fas-ang yearned to hear from her people back in Bisao, Bontoc. Had the *kaingins* been planted with *camote* and corn? Her kinsmen had heard of her delivering a child, and they sent a boy-cousin to inquire about her. He was told to see if Fas-ang lived happily, and if her Japanese husband really treated her well. If not, they would do him harm. The Bontocs, or *busol*, are very fierce...

The cousin came. Tanabata entertained the cousin well. He bought short pants for the Igorot boy and told him to do away with his G-string. The boy was much pleased. After a week, the boy said he would go back. And Tanabata bought some more clothes for him.

Fas-ang saw her cousin off. (Tanabata was in the shed house, cultivating the seedlings). She instructed him well. "Tell *Ama* and *Ina* I am happy here. They must not worry about me. My husband is kind, and I'm never in want. Give them this little money that I have saved for them. You see, I have a child, so I shall live here a long, long time yet. But I do wish I could go home sometime and see *Ama* and *Ina*. Often I feel homesick."

She wept. And when her cousin saw her tears, he wept too. Then they parted.

It was no hidden truth that Tanabata loved his wife dearly. In every way, he tried to show his affection. Once, he had not allowed her to go to the city to see the movies. But he repented afterwards and sent her there without her asking.

Fas-ang soon became a *cine* addict. She went to shows with one of the garden boys. Sometimes, she took her baby along. She carried the baby on her back. They had to take a kerosene lamp with them to light their way, coming home. They would return near midnight.

Tanabata, alone, would stay at home. He sat up, reading his books, Japanese novels. When Fas-ang arrived, she would be garrulous with what she had seen. Tanabata would tuck her under the thick blankets to warm her cold feet. She would then easily fall asleep, and after she had dozed off, he would himself retire.

More and more, Fas-ang liked to attend the shows. The city was two miles away. But that did not matter. The theater was fascinating. Moreover, Fas-ang admitted, she often met several of her relatives and townspeople in the theater. They, too, had learned to frequent the *cine*. Together they had a good time.

Tanabata asked Okamoto what he thought of Fas-ang's frequenting the shows. Okamoto, being less prosperous and more conservative, did not favor it. He advised Tanabata to stop her. But Tanabata was too indulgent with Fas-ang even to intimate such a thing to her. Though inclined to be cautious, he loved her too much to deny her any pleasure she desired.

Thus Fas-ang, after the day's duties, would run off to the show. Tanabata had grown even more lenient. He could never muster courage to restrain her, much less scold her. She never missed a single change of program in the theater. Tanabata did not know what to do with her. He could not understand what drew her to the *cine*. For his part, he was wholly uninterested in the screen shows; he had attended but once and that a long time ago, and he had been disgusted. Still Fas-ang continued to attend them as devotedly as ever.

One night she did not come home. She returned in the morning. Tanabata asked where she had slept, and she said, "With my cousin at the Campo Filipino." She had felt too lazy to walk all the way down to the valley, she said.

That whole day she remained at home. Tanabata went

out to the garden. Fas-ang rummaged among her things. She tied them into a bundle which she hid in the corner and dressed her child.

Then, at midnight, when Tanabata was sound asleep, she escaped. She carried her child and ran down the road where her lover was waiting. They would return to Bontoc, their native place. The man had been dismissed from the military post at Camp John Hay.

Fas-ang left a note on the table before she left. It had been written by the man who had seduced her. It read: *Do not follow us. We are returning home to Bontoc. If you follow us you will be killed on the way!*

When Tanabata had the letter read to him, he dared not pursue the truant lovers. The note was too positive to mean anything but death if disobeyed. He was grieved. And for three days, he could hardly eat. He felt bitter, being betrayed and deserted. Helpless, he was full of hatred for the man who had lured his wife away.

Okamoto, faithful indeed, came to comfort his friend. He offered to come with his wife and live with Tanabata. But Tanabata would not consider the proposition. Nor could he be comforted. He politely begged his friends to leave him alone. He had suddenly become gloomy. He sat in his hut all day and drank liquor. He shut himself in. The truck garden was neglected.

Months passed. The rows of cabbages were rotting, Tanabata was thought to be crazy. He did not care what happened to the plants. He had dismissed the few helpers that were left him. Weeds outgrew the seedlings. The rainy season set in, and the field was devastated by a storm. Tanabata lived on his savings.

The rainy season passed. Sunny, cold November came to the hills. In a month more, Tanabata would perhaps go home to die in Japan. His despondency had not been lessened. When he thought of his lost boy, he wept all the more.

Then, one evening, Fas-ang came back. She stood behind the house, surveying the wreck left of what was formerly a blooming garden. She had heard back home, from wayfarers who had returned, of Tanabata. The man who had stolen the affections of Fas-ang had left her.

"Your Japanese husband is said to be ruining himself," some reported.

"He pines for you and his boy," others brought back.

"It is said he is thinking of going home across the sea, but he must see his little son first," still others had told her.

Fas-ang at once decided. "Then I must return to him before it is too late." And so she came.

In the twilight, she stood, uncertain, hesitant. She heard the low mournful tune arising from the bamboo flute that Tanabata was playing. What loneliness! Fas-ang wondered if that now seemingly forbidding house was still open to her. Could she disperse the gloom that had settled upon it? There was a woman's yearning in her. But she wavered in her resolve, feeling ashamed.

The music had ceased. She almost turned away when the child, holding her hand, cried aloud. Tanabata looked out of the window, startled. He saw the mother and child. He rushed outside, exultant. Gently, he took them by their hands and led them into the house. Then he lighted the big lamp that had long hung from the ceiling, unused.

Sinai C. Hamada, born in 1912, in Baguio City, of a Japanese father and a Ibaloy native of Baguio, graduated from the University of the Philippines in 1937 with degrees in philosophy and law. He has practiced law since 1938 and been the editor of the Baguio Midland Courier *from 1947 to 1984 and the editor of the* Baguio Cordillera Post *from 1984 to date. He has published short stories, been active in community affairs, and taught law for several years. He has received national recognition in creative writing, community journalism and civic participation. He is also the person who has traveled the most over the Cordillera region on foot, horseback, riverboat, motor vehicle and by plane.*

"From that point on he linked himself with his oldest
and most venerable tradition, the one that to us
seemed anachronistic and contradictory to his
image as a refined Western man."

The Masterpiece

BY PALOMA DÍAZ-MAS

IN spite of all appearances, Amal was an island in our world.
At first glance, he looked like the stereotype of a ladies' man, a
somewhat old-fashioned dandy. But behind his suits of impeccable
cut (English wool in the winter and alpaca or linen in the
summer), behind his Italian shoes and silk ties, behind his
handkerchiefs embroidered with an A that swirled in off-white
scrolls, behind his polite, brilliant conversation, behind his
prematurely gray sideburns and impeccable beard, behind his
aristocratic hands that were never tinged yellow from nicotine,
behind his education at a couple of American unversities,
behind his art studies in Italy and Germany, behind his fluency
in four or five Western languages, behind his masculine cologne
and his billfold bulging with credit cards, behind all these signs
in which he had adopted the most genteel, dazzling, and even
snobbish styles of Europe and part of America, there were
hidden feelings, convictions, and a morality that seemed to all

of us to be hereditary, almost anachronistic, and, above all, incomprehensible in a man like him.

We only knew bits and pieces about his life: a passing reference to a rich, elderly father who, from some small and faraway desert land—such a little country that we could never remember its name—punctually sent sizable checks to the institutions charged with the long intellectual and artistic preparation of his son (a preparation that started in an English adolescence and continued almost into his cosmopolitan forties). There were vague evocations of the diverse habits, customs, and landscapes that he knew; and always we were convinced that any time we mentioned a country, a city, a monument, or a river, Amal had been there, had strolled its streets, gazed at its architecture, and had walked along its banks.

He developed his art with the same aristocratic nonchalance with which he carried on a sophisticated conversation or undertook a trip to a distant country. And, in spite of that—or perhaps because of that—he was one of the painters most in demand at the time. Dealers fought over him; art galleries and public institutions were eager to award him prizes or commission his works. There was no technique whose secrets he did not know: with equal skill he did sketchings or engravings or worked in color. Oil paints and tempera, red crayon and silver pencil, chalk and stylus, all yielded with docility to his pictorial knowledge. At first he turned his attention to landscapes, somehow implacable in spite of their pleasant surface; then, seemingly tired of them, he immersed himself in hyper-realistic still lifes, impressive in their vivid anguish; finally he drifted to a non-figurative style of enormous expressive force: sometimes undulating lines like waves or serpents filled his paintings with frenetic motion, while others were labyrinthian swarms of diminutive geometric forms that, by intertwining and intersecting, captured the viewer in a suggestive maze that seemed to contain figures where there were none.

From that point on he linked himself with his oldest and most venerable tradition, the one that to us seemed anachronistic and contradictory to his image as a refined Western man; his paintings became more and more filled with cursive and elegant lines that, without being Kufic script, strongly reminded one of the writing that decorated the marble and stucco facades of the palaces, mosques, and madrasahs of his native land. And the backgrounds had progressively acquired the tonality of marble, or the relief of reddish leather, or embellishments of gold and silver like the swirls that illuminate medieval Korans, or metallic iridescence like that of heretical Persian fabrics.

Indeed for him, in spite of their beauty, they were heretical, those dark blue and green tapestries that neatly paraded whole armies, half-veiled maidens, earthly monsters, and fantastic birds, and that even dared to depict the Prophet himself, carried off from heaven by a flying horse with human face, or descending into the seven circles of the inferno via a ladder no man had ever trod. Because Amal, the artist in vogue at art auctions and salons, was a devout believer and strict Moslem. Precisely for this reason, he had never painted a human figure and declared he never would.

Once someone tried to make a joke of it: How was it possible that he, a cultured and educated man, an inspired and well-trained painter, could renounce figurative art just because of a superstition, a prohibition dictated by the Koran thirteen centures before in order to avert idolatry and now totally devoid of meaning? Amal's eyes glistened in anger and scorn, his fingers tightened on the glass of juice he was drinking—it was, I think, the cocktail celebrating the opening of his fifth one-man exposition—and for a moment we all feared there would be a disagreeable scene. But nothing happened. The violence-charged silence that followed was enough so that our unwise companion slipped away and left the group unnoticed. No one ever made such an observation to Amal again. Nevertheless, after that episode, which everyone else doubtless forgot, I became convinced—quite irrationally, without any real basis for my thoughts—that at heart Amal wanted to paint a figure and, what's more, that perhaps he was already trying it in secret.

Time passed and I forgot that idea, which had crossed my mind a time or two like a falling star. And when I had already forgotten it, Amal came to see me.

He was caught up in an agitation that was unusual for him, always such a controlled person. I had never seen him so excited, so ill at ease. Stammering, for the first time upset and unsure of himself, he confessed everything to me: he had spent years working on the project and had finally accomplished it, but I should say nothing to anyone. It had taken a great effort for him to decide, he had destroyed the finished work a number of times, he had had many doubts and constant pangs of conscience, and now he believed he had finally found a solution. He had intended to keep it secret; I was the only person he had told about it. He realized he could not hide it, he needed someone else's opinion, someone able to keep a secret, to judge it but never talk about it. It was essential that I give him my opinion, a single opinion would be enough, but he needed at least one. He would only let me see it once and—he repeated—I should not tell anyone about it.

Naturally he had painted a human figure.

He took me to a place where I had never been: a little garret in an old section of the city. It was a single small room, but very well lit thanks to a window that opened out onto a sea of greenish tile roofs. It had a strong smell of paint and turpentine, the unmistakable smells of a studio where a painter had been working many months. Amal's workshop that we all knew was at the opposite side of the city, and it was obvious that this one had been, until then, his other place, his secret refuge.

There was a painting hanging on the back wall, facing the window. When I looked at it, I wondered if my friend had gone crazy, or if he was simply making fun of me: it was a beautiful painting, no doubt, with a special harmony in the movement of the lines and a delightful sensitivity in the combination of the various tones from the full spectrum of terracotta and pink. But it was not figurative, there was no body, no face: just an amalgam of colored brush strokes.

I looked at him in surprise. But before I was able to mutter a word, Amal motioned that I should sit down in front of the painting on a large cushion on the floor; and, having recovered his usual serene and imperturbable aura of the perfect gentleman, he whispered to me, gently and ironically: "How can we enjoy beauty unless we have the virtue of patience?" Once he had said this phrase, which sounded to me like the aphorism of a wise Moslem much older than he, he left me alone, face to face with the painting.

Hours went by as I immersed myself in that maze of undulating lines and delicate colors that had, I don't know why, a charm I dared then to describe—without realizing just how correctly—as erotic. The sun began to set and a reddish glow, emanating from the clouds on the horizon above the waves of the rooftops, began to enter the window. First it was like a vermilion beam, and then the room became colored with an unreal rosy tint that seemed to set the walls themselves throbbing with life and blood.

Then I saw her: a woman, nude, gently reclining, with her hands resting softly in her lap. The rosy skin that seemed to palpitate was scarcely distinguishable from her hair with its reddish glow, or from her reddish pubic hair. Her rouged cheeks almost blended into the color of her hair, and against her rosy skin one could barely see her light scarlet lips. She seemed to burn in her resting position, like an incandescent and feverish rose. She was the most fantastically beautiful woman I had ever seen.

My view of her could last but a few minutes: only as long as the sunset. Because gradually the rosy light of the setting sun turned violet and then a deep, dense blue, and as these changes occurred, her beauty dissolved into an amalgam of confused brush strokes until the figure sank into the canvas like a coin that one throws into a deep pond: it becomes smaller and smaller, more and more diffuse among the metallic waves that it forms, until there remains only a distant glimmer and then, suddenly, the glimmer disappears before our very eyes and we see it no more.

And I saw her no more. Because Amal never showed her to me again.

He hardly paid attention to my mumbled words of ineffable enthusiasm: he was so sure that she was perfect that perhaps he did not need an opinion, just a witness.

I think no one else saw her, although the painting was on display a long time: first in the most prestigious art gallery in the city, under implacable spotlights that were incapable of revealing its mystery. It sold for a good price, and I believe the buyer was a bank that installed the painting like a jewel in the lobby of its main office. There she doubtless remains, silent and hidden, the most beautiful woman I have ever seen: in a place where the incandescent light of the sunset never enters.

Born in 1954, in Madrid, Paloma Díaz-Mas is a university professor whose area of scholarly specialization is the language and literature of the Sephardic Jews. As a creative writer she has published novels, a play and a collection of short stories, Nuestro milenio, *in which "The Masterpiece" appeared.* Nuestro milenio *was the runner-up for Spain's national literature prize in 1986. The dazzling translation is by Phyllis Zatlin, a professor of Spanish in the USA.*

"If you achieved what you were saying, you wouldn't have gotten angry, you'd have accepted his remarks magnanimously."

The Deck Chair

BY ALI ELMAK

YOU went to your office regularly each morning. A precise timepiece. That's what you were. You'd get there at 8:00 a.m., winter and summer. You never changed this habit of yours whether you were working in El Damer or El Fasher or in Kassala. Just think: you've served in most of the regions of your country, but don't know what the differences are. In the office during the day; at night, in the club. And always there's a merchant and a colleague, and a butcher, and a barber, and a stern director (or a lenient one) and...and...

And now, here's the capital: your hometown. You came back after a lot of moving around; you worked here for a year or part of a year until retirement "overtook" you. You say retirement "overtook you" just as death might "overtake" people. But isn't retirement a kind of death? Doesn't it mean your usefulness is over—just as life is over? Isn't it true that living is working? This is the first day of the last vacation of all; from now on, you won't wake up early. You won't head for the office and be there at 8:00 a.m. You went there by taxi so often you knew every inch of the way by heart: the street, the lampposts, George's cafe, the movie advertisements. They're always changing, but everything else stays the same. The White Nile bridge. What a pleasure to doze in the car as it approaches it. And how cool the air becomes as it passes over the surface of the river so that a refreshing moisture envelopes you and sends you to sleep. But you've aged, and you don't have a car. At least you've got a house! What will you do now?

"Good-bye, my dear Fadl, we certainly learned a lot from you! We'll miss you a lot, too!" This is what a fellow worker said. And you knew he was lying. After all, his future in the service was linked to your retirement. What hypocrisy! Did he even bother to hide his malicious smile? This son of a...! But retirement's the death that will catch up with you all. For every stage of a man's life there's an appropriate saying. For this one, condolences are appropriate...but you're insincere yourself. If you believed what you were saying, you wouldn't have gotten angry, you'd have accepted his remarks magnanimously.

Were you really loved and respected? Do you remember your severity and rigor? And your stock query, "Why are you late? Were you asleep? Ah!...Did the soft morning air sweeten your slumber? Or maybe a bit too much strong wine last night?" Remarks like these would gall the office workers but they kept silent, afraid of the consequences. You, meanwhile, feared the director. Every boss has a boss. When he'd look over at you, or summon you, you'd break into a sweat...your mouth would get dry...He actually said, "Oh my dear Fadl, we'll miss you!" The dirty dog! The man can't even write a letter or a memorandum! He didn't observe the good English precedents; good heavens! Just think of Smith, Jones and Randall! But as far as he's concerned...he couldn't care less if the entire service headed for a complete collapse. And where are we now compared with those days? Finished, by God!

Today the bosses are college boys! "Remember, Mr. Fadl,

different men for different times!" That kid was always saying this to you. He was the same age as your own son but he was educated. But what an education! Oversleeping in the University campus, stuffing on lentils and beans, lying back in the lecture hall, or the coffee shop. Next a university degree! And then you see them going in leaps and bounds up the bureaucratic ladder! Great God in heaven! "Were you ever his boss, my dear Fadl?" No. First you had the English until they left the country, then came the college boys.

It's known that in the town of Omdurman, the sun's a blazing fire. After 8:00 a.m., it sets coffee shops aboil. It's unendurable. People take refuge in offices with fans or air conditioners. This is not because they are at all disposed to work, but because they long only for cool air and relaxation. You feel...maybe for the first time, that it's death to stay in these houses but you can't leave the neighborhood. Doesn't a job seem a merciful reprieve to you mother of all these children? This fruitful, fertile woman...she's like the Nile delta itself! If there's no way out, then better sit by the street in the shade: read the morning newspaper, watch the pedestrians and cars stream by...Where can they all be going? When you took the deck chair from the storeroom and brushed off the dust of years, the motes reminded you of the times in Al Fasher where it was made, and five other chairs...all of which got smashed leaving only this one. The chair, a chicken sold for five piastres, and the prisoner making it was strained and taut as he bent intent on his task. He strained his back so that the officials both British and Sudanese might rest their backsides. All admired his art and his skill. A skill stemming from the marriage of patience and compulsion. The chair's striped red and yellow fabric and white-painted wood thoroughly charmed them. "Perhaps your maker was a murderer or a thief or a rapist; maybe you'll die, and the chair will remain. Think of all the thieves and rapists running around free, pleased with themselves...Heavy dust flies out at each blow."

When you were fashioned, oh deck chair, a chicken sold for five piastres, and a lamb for fifty. The army barracks were full of women and wine; in the rainy season, the irrigation canals would fill to overflowing, and a green carpet of herbage would spread over the hills. At other times you'd see boys drinking from the water holes with horses and donkeys, water was scarce, and Atiyma would make wine and you'd drink most of it. You'd eat half a lamb, and wasn't it the best thing your wife ever did when she refused to stay in Al Fasher! In leaving your bed, she didn't leave it empty. There was Su'ad, the Fezzani girl. And you were the chief clerk. Those were the days, my deck chair! Now you've grown old...me, too.

And there you are sitting in the chair in the shade, you're looking out at the street and the people in it. You stretch out your legs, and as the shade does combat with the sun, you hear:

"Mr. Fadl, good morning! Are you all right?"

"Sure...fine..."

"You're not sick?"

"Not at all."

"You're on vacation then?"

"Yes."

"That's great. Are you thinking of making a trip?"

"No."

"Good! Soon the rains will come and the weather will get better."

Why does your neighbor insist on all this talk? Or is this the way shopkeepers talk? God damn them! And the neighbor went on:

"That's really great, my dear Fadl. When does your vacation end?"

"This is my final leave."

"Oh my gosh...You're not going back to work then...Good Lord! What a shame!"

The face of the cherished neighbor changed subtly. Its bright and cheerful appearance became overcast. His features stiffened; he pressed his lips together, and frowned. Or at least this is how it looked to you.

You say to yourself, "You poor man, Fadl. Is retirement

really death? Here you are, competent and capable and in good health...except for coughing fits which leave you choking and short of breath. You could work until you're a hundred."

The cherished neighbor went away. You see him shaking his head regretfully; in the neighbor's eyes, you were something... now you're nothing. You were the much-esteemed chief clerk...and now! Esteem is gone, replaced by sympathy and condolence. The cars stream by. Where are the people going? Do they all work? Or are they bored with life at home? Have they wives and children, too. To hell with the old woman. She still uses perfumes and looks after her appearance...on an endless day like this she might tempt you...you might weaken and give in. It is better to sit here in the shade than to be home.

Car horns echo and re-echo across the street. Just look at the cars and the congestion. For the first time you notice this old street has gone untouched by repair; things, it seems, haven't changed as they should have. Is this really your first day? Is this how you'll spend the rest of your life? Or what's left of it? You served out your time with the government then it kicked you into the street. Here you sit talking to yourself. Street scenes recur; people come and go; the cars make you dizzy. What's government work after all? Isn't it a one-day exercise repeated for thirty or forty years? Suddenly, your train of thought is broken:

"Al-salaam Alaykum."

The voice is hesitant. You give a start and open your eyes wide. You stare at the man who greeted you and answer, "Wa alaykum al-salaam Mr."

What do you want to say to him? Do you know him? Who is this man? Any number of people will say "Al-salaam alaykum" to you. They'll greet you this way even if you're asleep. Anyhow, you don't know him. Such a greeting, they say, was hallowed by the Prophet; that's why these people follow the custom. The passer-by took your greeting positively. He walked on, saying: "Praise the Lord! Praise his holy name! Watch and wait! There is no power and no strength save in

God! All of you! Listen and heed! There is no...the Lord...Oh you..."

Shouts! And then a truck loaded with soldiers, all of them with red berets, runs over a little girl who was crossing the street. You jump to your feet. The deck chair falls back as if resting itself now that your weight is removed. Where did the people come from? In the twinkling of an eye! How did people crowd around so quickly? Wasn't the street half empty? Listen to the voices clamoring in your ear:

"Army trucks always go too fast. The driver was wrong. No doubt about that! My God!"

"Not at all. You're wrong! The girl was at fault. She didn't stop to see the street was clear."

"But she's dead!"

"How could she be dead without a mark on her?"

"That's usually the way it is these days!"

"Will the law punish the driver of the truck?"

The soldiers with their red berets had begun to jump down from the back of the truck. You peer between heads and shoulders and necks; there's the child thrown on the side of the road. She wore a green dress. She'd been carrying a book whose pages were scattered all around. On them were drawings of animals and large colored letters; an exercise book was jammed under a tire of the truck. You couldn't get it out. Her face was flecked with blood. Death had closed her eyes. And you recognized him; death. "My God! How could this poor child die on her way to school? Praise God for having preserved you on this earth for more than half a century! And here an earnest little girl dies without a reason!"

There's a babble of voices:

"That's the way it is these days."

"Get something to cover her with."

"Take her to the hospital!"

"A doctor should look at her."

"But she's dead!"

"Who's to blame then? The driver or the brakes or those soldiers? What about the red berets?"

"Come on let's move on before the police come and you're blamed for the killing."

The driver's hands clung to the steering wheel. He had turned away from it trying to hide his face, while the soldiers cordoned off the spectators.

And now the shade retreats in the face of the sun's continued aggression. The sun continues to climb. There's nothing left to do now but go home. So take your chair and lean it carefully against the wall as if you wanted it to rest after its exertions. You lie down on the bed. The day is silent now; it's just been fed with the blood of the child; maybe your wife will look in on you after awhile? Where is Hell to be found? In the street? Or at home? Well...let's wait for the second day of your new life.

Born in 1937, in Omdurman, Sudan, Ali Elmak studied at the University of Khartoum and the University of Southern California, and was a Fulbright scholar at the University of New Mexico. He has published and edited many works in Arabic, including five collections of short stories. He is a university professor and the President of the Sudanese Writers' Union. This story was translated from Arabic by the former U.S. Ambassador to Sudan, Hume Alexander Horan.

"She got it in her head that if she could cook him goat water like mine, that would do the trick."

Goat Water

BY BARBARA GILSON

ME and Lucinda, we been friends all our lives. Born on the same part of the island, houses just across the trees from each other; grow up here too, on the west coast of Dominica, 'bout halfway from Roseau to Portsmouth, in Coulibistri. Her daddy and mine both fishermen. Some of the men in the village went, when we were little, to work in the coconut factory, but my papa said he die if he have to stay indoors all the day, and Lucinda's father say the same. So they went out every morning in the boats with the nets, and came home when the sun going down.

All the men in the village do that, and when they have a good day with the fish, you hear them before you see them, coming home from the sea; they yelling and shouting in the boats. The sun going down is so bright you can't see nothing but the light hitting off the water like lightning on land. We hear the voices, and then the boats start out of the light, just dark shapes, coming closer to land until you see the shape of the men too.

My daddy always start to wave his arm from far out, and when we saw that, me and Lucinda, we start to run down from the hill across the sand. We'd wait all nervous while the men beached the boats and hauled out the catch. The women were there to sort it, some for home, some for the market in town. Then Lucinda and me, we ran to our fathers to be hugged and put up on their shoulders and carried home for dinner. Even when the day bad, my daddy told me it seemed good when I came to meet him.

We went to the same school, the primary school down in the village. My family house and Lucinda's too, they a ways up in the hills. My father built the house himself, and he put it among the trees where the forest start, so it always be a little cool. Every morning Lucinda and me would run out of the forest and through the village, racing to see who get to school first. Sometimes I won, but mostly she did. Lucinda always real fast on her feet.

We didn't like school much. Too full of the devil we were, my mother always said. It was too dreary every day, reading the same thing, doing sums, writing letters so many times, and then, if they weren't right, having to do them over five extra times. Miss Lord, the teacher, she studied in England, and she always wanted everything just so. Some days we wouldn't go to school after we left home. We'd double back and go on down to the shore. Nobody be there except a couple of old ladies, fixing the nets. The men all out to sea and the women in their houses or gardens. We'd spend the day fishing or working on the nets or diving off the dock and go home before our daddies came back. Miss Lord used to get real mad when we ran off like that. Said we'd come to no good.

Other times we run up back into the forest and swim in the mountain river. Up there it stays cool and the water cold, but sweet. It gives you a jolt when you jump in, but then it feel good. We lie on the rocks and let the water pour over us. When you look up there's only the palms over you like a high, high ceiling, with little openings in the leaves that let in fine slivers of sun.

We made plans for our lives there too. We both wanted to marry fishermen, not anybody from the factory, and we wanted good cricketers, somebody who played on the all-island team, a real strong man.

I went to the school four years; then my mamma said I could stop and stay at home to help her. I felt real good about that, getting into life like a grown woman. Lucinda, she kept going to school four more years; she was quick, didn't have any trouble with reading or writing or numbers, except that a lot of times, she was flighty. Miss Lord said that Lucinda was the smartest child, boy or girl, she'd ever taught on the island, and told her she should try for the grammar school, that she could maybe even think about university later on. There'd never been a girl on Dominica who'd done that, and not many boys, except from the town families with money.

Lucinda liked the idea of going away and all the attention Miss Lord paid her. She even started saying she didn't mind the studying and writing. She talked to me sometimes about going to England for university. That made me feel strange, the thought of her going so far and learning so many things.

But all the talk come to an end when she met Carlton Hibbert. He came from Portsmouth, and one night he came to one of the dances they had outside of town every Saturday. Lucinda and me were between thirteen and fourteen, and we'd just started going. I was a shy girl, and hardly could say a word to anybody. Lucinda got her growth early. She was tall and pretty and lively, and she knew how to play the boys like a fisherman with his net. She didn't have to learn how; someway she just knew. They were always inviting her to walk out, and she always said yes and no at once, and they'd keep coming to ask her some more. Sometimes she would go to the movies with one, but she knew how to hold them off wherever she was.

Carlton Hibbert was as good-looking for a man as Lucinda be for a woman. And he owned his own taxi. He worked on the boats in Portsmouth fishing, but he had been a sailor too and put money aside so he could get the taxi. When times were good he went out on the boats, and other times he went to the airport to meet the planes. Sometimes he got real tourists who wanted to see the island, and he'd take them around all day.

He had plenty of women, but Lucinda did something special to him. He tried to play with her, but she played with him too. She fall in love with Carlton, but she not too dumb to play with him. He was different from the other boys, and she wanted him bad; she never let him know how much she like him, and there was always somebody else around after her. Finally Carlton put up a house in the forest near where we lived and asked Lucinda to move in. Everybody was surprised she got him so good. They had a baby in a year or so, and two more later on.

After a while I wasn't so shy as before and I got to look more womanly. And I got my own man, a good man. I was near fifteen when Damon Anthony took an interest in me. He like most to be on the sea. He born in our village and start out fishing with his father, but then he went to work on the cargo boats going up and down the islands, sometimes as far as Puerto Rico.

He come home one time after being on the sea three months, and we noticed each other. We always knew each other, but this time we took notice. He start to visit my house when he was home, and bring me things back from his journeys. He was lively and loved to dance, and he could make anybody laugh with the mad stories he told about his traveling and the things he saw. When he came off the ship at Roseau he'd catch a ride right to my house and call to me when he was still down the road. Then I'd stop whatever I was doing and run out the door to meet him halfway. My mother always laughed and told me Damon had made me crazy.

One time he even took me on board for one of his trips out, the only time I've ever been off the island. The boat went down to Martinique that time, and Damon took me into Fort-de-France, bought me some perfume and a necklace. But there were so many people there, standing around on the dock, walking up and down the streets, going in and out of the shops, I felt like I couldn't breathe. It was a pretty town, with a big church, and town hall, so many shops and eating places, but it was too wild and full. I feel better up in the forest where it's quiet or down on the shore where I know everybody.

Damon had his own house, and he fixed it up more, put in a bigger kitchen and a bedroom. He did this before he asked me to live with him, to show he was serious about me. My mother was happy, and even my father think well of Damon.

So Lucinda and me were both married and still friends. We did our work together, went to market together, and when our men were home we went to parties and picnics and Carnival together. My daughter born a year after I move in with Damon, and our kids always together too.

One thing we did each for ourselves was cook. We had a kind of friends' war about who was the best cook, and that was one thing I was better at. Not a lot, but enough. Lucinda did her mountain chicken, and I did mine. We hunted them up in the hills together, but the seasonings and tastings we did most secret in our kitchens. The same with tannia soup and salt fish in chemise, and baigner, and more than anything with the goat water.

In February there's *Carnival,* and all over the island you have parades and picnics and a lot of dancing. And cricket matches, one village playing another. It turned out both Lucinda and me got one girlhood wish, because Damon and Carlton were both good batsmen. Carlton was really fine. A couple of times he went to play in the Test Matches. And every *Carnival* time, Damon and Carlton played for the village.

For the women there was a competition too: to see who could cook the best goat water. We started, Lucinda and me, when we were about seventeen; my mother was one of the winners nearly every year, and there were a couple of other older women who won. Then after a few years I came in second, and the next year after that first. For one thing, I raised my own goat right from the moment it was born, but I spent much time too searching out spices and mixing them up, getting the taste like I want them. Couldn't nobody else figure just what I did. I went up into the forest for roots, and put them together over and over different ways, until the tang came through just right. I always had a way with growing things, and I could graft plants and bring out new herb like the old one, and a little different too. One of my best I called the blue root, because the leaf looked a little blue over the green in the middle of the forest, when the light came down through the palms.

Lucinda did some good cooking and mixing too. In fifteen years of the Carnival Competition either she or I won almost always, me nine times, Lucinda, five. One year Victoria Farquhar won, but that was an early year, when Lucinda and me did more dancing than cooking. After that we paid more attention.

Lucinda had her three babies, but for a long time after my daughter was born I didn't have any others. That was a heavy sadness for me. I would have liked many children, and at least one more, a boy to call Damon Junior. After we were together ten years, though, I started another child. It was a boy, but very weak, and he only lived three weeks. That made me nearly die myself, but Damon comforted me and stayed with me, leaving going off to sea for nearly five months.

Lucinda's three were getting big, and so was my girl. I got a little heavy, but Lucinda hardly changed at all, except for her clothes. She kept up with all the styles. She was always lively, but then, about four years ago I could tell that something was changed, she was so turned about, she just wasn't herself. She finally told me that Carlton was up to something, seeing another woman, not just fooling around, but steady. And one day Lucinda found all his clothes and things gone. They told her down at Roseau that he'd left the island with the woman on one of the morning boats.

For a long time she was like someone crazy. She start going out at night with this man and that man, and drinking. She would go off to Portsmouth or Roseau for days and leave the children, but they were almost like mine anyway, so it wasn't a problem. They stayed in our house. That was the only time Damon and me had a real falling out. He said Lucinda was no good, running around and disgracing her name and her family. I knew that wasn't right. I told him Lucinda was just mad with grief, acting wild to stop the pain, not really knowing what she was doing. I was sure she'd come back to herself. Some days she'd stay in bed in her house all day and I'd go over there talking to her and listening. I could tell she had to have time the way a broken leg needs time.

And she came back to herself. Stopped the running and the night-time life and began walking on the beach, working in her garden, talking again to me like before. She was maybe a little quieter, but most of the time she was Lucinda, quick-talking, always ready with a joke or back-chat for the men. They still came around even when she went back to her old ways; she was still the best-looking woman in the village.

Then one time, about a year and a half ago, my Damon's ship came back from a journey to St. Kitts, and when they were just coming into port, a storm hit. The boat went down with everyone on board. They found his body two days after.

Around then Lucinda took up with Harry Clemson. She'd been flirting with a lot of men for a couple years, but she like Harry. He was a really good man, reminded me a little of Damon. He was a steady man, but he laughed a lot too; always good for a party, but he worked hard. He and Lucinda were happy together, but somehow he didn't want to live with her. He came from Portsmouth, and we heard that he'd had a wife a long time ago who walked out on him, and he wasn't going to take a chance again.

Lucinda used to come to my house with him all the time,

to spend the evening or to take me out with them to town. She knew I was grieving, and she tried to ease me the way I helped her when Carlton left. She used to say besides, that Harry loved my goat water, that if she had just the way I had of putting the spices in, he probably would move into her house. I was still playing with my blue root, and a red pea I found, from high up in the forest, and the goat water was famous by now. I sold some of it from my house, and people would come from around the island to buy, even a tourist every now and then.

I lived alone too. My daughter turned sixteen and was a very flighty girl. She found a boy from Roseau who'd always been a rude one and started staying with him. A little while later they left Dominica, and I heard they'd gone up to St. Martin.

I set up a little stand next to my house, selling cangrejo, chicken calypso, and baigner along with the goat water. Mango fool and rum punch too. Lucinda told me I was a born business woman. She was starting to get more discontented with Harry. He wasn't so handsome as Carlton; he ran a bit to fat, but he had a smile and a way of talking that showed he was steady, and she wanted to have her life with him for good.

She would talk to me about how to convince him to move over to her house. Her children were well grown. Her oldest girl got married and went to her own house. Lucinda talked all the time about how we were past thirty-five and it was time to settle down for good.

"I've got all this room," she said. "Philip and Alicia be moving out pretty soon, too. It doesn't make sense for Harry to live all by himself and me all by myself."

She got it in her head that if she could cook him goat water like mine, that would do the trick. She began pestering me for the recipe. I'd won the competition five years running, and she was after me to tell her the things I did with the herbs. I said that now, especially, I couldn't let out my ways, since I was doing business, selling the goat water, so how could I give away my trade secrets?

But she said she'd never let anybody know, that it was only to cook in her own kitchen and only for Harry. She talked about all the years back we'd been friends, how we were in school together, found our men and lived our lives next to each other. So at last I told her I'd give her some of the herbs, and show her how they go into the stew, but I wouldn't tell her how to grow them herself. And I gave her some blue root, already prepared, and some of the red bean.

"You have to put in a little of the root, then a little of the bean, then taste," I said. "Then a little more root, a little more bean. There's no real set amount. It depend on the kind of meat and the strength of the clove, and all the rest of what's in the pot. You keep tasting until the goat water gets right. You eat what I cook all the time. You'll know when it's right.

I never saw Lucinda happier. I went over with her to get the goat water started. She stood by the kettle putting in the herbs and tasting. Tasting and putting in. And smiling. Later in the day, when Philip and Alicia came home, they found Lucinda lying dead next to the kitchen table. The doctor say she took a heart attack. I think she maybe used too much of the red bean.

Harry was really broken up for a while. He come to my house a lot, talk about Lucinda and tell me his grief. I've been feeding him up pretty good, and he's not as sad as he was; in fact, he's putting on a little more weight. I'm not as lonely as I used to be either. Harry's here almost all the time now, and he's taking a real interest in the business.

Since graduating from college, Barbara Gilson has served in several editorial positions in the book publishing industry. She also worked and lived in Bogota, Columbia; her knowledge of Spanish is masterful.
This story is one of a collection based on her experience and observation of life in Latin America and the Caribbean.

"Leaning against a wall, he abandoned himself to
another daydream in which he saw himselfas
the chief medicine man of Machupicchu..."

The Sacred
Number Seven

BY GERHART A. DRUCKER

"THIS was probably the Incas' funeral chamber, though some
archeologists believe it may have been a reception hall. You
see again the incredible craftsmanship of the stone masons,
who fitted the big rocks precisely one next to the other, row
upon row, without mortar. These walls have endured for
centuries, in spite of storms and earthquakes. Please look at
these niches, each big enough for a man to stand in. They
may have housed the mummies of deceased kings or noblemen.
Count the niches; there are seven. The Incas considered seven
a sacred number."

Alfred, who had sat down on a rock, barely listened to
Pedro's litany, and gave the walls and niches a cursory glance.
The other members of his travel group, his wife Becky among
them, had formed a semicircle around their dark-skinned young
guide, whose Spanish accent enhanced his flawless English. They
were typical tourists, each equipped with a camera, some

111

carrying field glasses, one man even lugging a tripod wherever he went. Becky, standing close to the guide, was scribbling furiously into her travel diary. For a moment Alfred's eyes rested on her slender figure, her attractive face framed by brown hair that fell to her shoulders from below her broad-brimmed hat. The polka-dotted blue blouse, red jacket, and matching slacks and sneakers had been his twentieth anniversary present to her, two weeks before their departure.

The semicircle dissolved; cameras clicked. If each shutter click sounded like a gunshot, a man would think he was watching a Western rather than visiting ruins, Alfred thought. Machupicchu was teeming with tourists. Bus upon crowded bus dumped its multilingual cargo in front of the ruins' entrance; visitors from every nook of the globe were swarming all over the remains of chambers, temples, patios, and staircases of the Incas' famous mountain bastion in southern Peru.

Alfred raised his camera to take a photo, then changed his mind. No doubt Becky had photographed whatever there was worth seeing. Driven by compulsion, she had taken many hundreds of photos on this trip: lakes and volcanoes, street scenes, Indian markets, baroque church portals, herds of llamas and alpacas, and now film upon film of Inca ruins. Ancient stones fascinated her; Alfred was more interested in living people. His concern for human beings, and compassion for their suffering, had motivated him thirty years earlier to choose medicine for his career.

As he was sitting there, a black-haired man of small frame, in his early fifties, wearing brown slacks and a maroon nylon jacket, a camera slung over his shoulder, he looked like any tourist taking a rest. He needed one, because he had seen enough of ruins and artifacts. He yearned to meet the people of this land, the descendants of the Indians who had built Machupicchu, to talk with them, listen to their problems, watch them at work. The day before, in Cusco, while the others were laughing over their cocktails, he had walked all over the Plaza de Armas and observed the people. Stoic-faced Quechua women with black hats, sitting behind tables loaded with fruit, vegetables, and colorful woven goods, had vied for his attention. Barefoot children had surrounded him, tugging at his sleeves, begging, and he had given each one a coin, till his pockets were empty. In the cathedral he had watched worshippers deeply absorbed in their prayers, while unsmiling saints looked down at them from gilded altars. He had strayed into a centuries-old courtyard, where the dead past and the somnolent present hovered over a little girl asleep on the lowest step of a worn staircase.

Pedro talked on and on; Becky continued her relentless note-taking. Alfred shut his eyes and tried to imagine how the inhabitants of Machupicchu had actually lived. In his daydream he saw hordes of half-naked, brawny Indians building retention walls for their terraces, sweat streaming from their foreheads and backs under the brutal sun; women weaving alpaca wool into all kinds of lovely patterns; and farmers tilling the terraced fields, where they raised maize and potatoes in hundreds of varieties.

Becky's call dispelled his daydream; she had clambered into one of the niches and wanted him to take her picture. He obliged her, then caught her in his arms as she was stepping down. Her high-pitched, widely audible whisper dashed his surge of affection.

"Why do you daydream all the time, Alfred? You ought to listen to what the guide is telling us. After all, you paid a lot for this trip."

Indeed he had; and he also was still paying the price for a mistake he had made years ago.

The guide moved on, leading his charges over a rocky staircase to the next obligatory stop in their two-hour tour. Becky, as always, stayed close to him, eager not to miss one word of his sermon. Alfred lagged behind; on the top step he turned around to take in the glorious view.

He was standing amidst the ruins of a citadel built on top of a cliff one thousand five hundred feet about the Urubamba River, a natural moat surrounding the cliff on three sides. Untold numbers of Indians, the Incas' subjects, had labored centuries ago to divide the cliff's flanks into terraces, each a cultivated field. Verdant mountains rose steeply on both sides of the winding "Sacred River of the Incas," while in the background the rocky pyramid of Huyana Picchu towered hundreds of feet above the ruins.

The others had gone ahead; Alfred felt no urge to follow. Leaning against a wall, he abandoned himself to another daydream in which he saw himself as the chief medicine man of Machupicchu, attending an Inca nobleman's wife who had fallen ill with shaking chills, chest pain, hacking cough, and rusty sputum. Oh, for an ampule of Penicillin, but this drug lay still half a millenium in the future. He had to use herbs, incantations, and prayer (much as doctors the world over would have to do for lobar pneumonia until the advent of antibiotics). When the noblewoman died, her furious husband ordered the medicine man to be beheaded. Alfred felt an unpleasant sensation in the back of his neck. Quickly he shifted to another daydream, the one that had haunted him time and again since medical school days. In this dream he was the physician-in-chief of a hospital in a primitive country somewhere in deepest Asia or Africa, where day after day, without recourse to specialists, he had to apply every last bit of his skill and knowledge to save lives, in the operating room, on the wards and in the clinic. He envisioned himself in a white gown, stethoscope in pocket, administering to loinclothed men and their bare-bosomed wives and daughters, or performing difficult operations, assisted by bright young natives whom he had taught the basics of asepsis and anesthesia. He, Alfred, a second Albert Schweitzer. But...

Two groups of tourists had passed Alfred, who had caught snatches of French and German; now a third group was coming up the stairway. Realizing that he had lost his group, he ran ahead, past the Germans and the French, to catch up with his tripmates in an odd-shaped courtyard where Pedro, like a priest, was intoning with biblical solemnity:

"Count the corners. They are another example of the sacred number seven."

When Becky spied her husband, she interrupted her note-taking and addressed him in a biting whisper that could be heard in each sacred corner:

"Here you are at last. I was getting worried about you. What were you doing? Daydreaming as usual, no doubt."

He didn't answer; instead, like a model tourist, he counted the corners. "One, two, three..."

Night fell during the four-hour train ride back to Cusco. Alfred, sitting next to his sleeping wife, tried to read, but couldn't concentrate. His thoughts drifted back to their first date, when he had been a senior in medical school and she a lab technician at the University Hospital. Though shy with women, he had asked her for a date on a dare from one of his classmates, and to his surprise she had accepted. At dinner at the Red Lion he had told her of his plans of going to an underdeveloped country; she had said nothing, other than to complain about the toughness of her steak. After sitting through *South Pacific* he had taken her home; a perfunctory kiss; "Thanks for the beautiful evening." But again he was surprised when she agreed to another date.

She was very pretty: big brown eyes, shoulder-length brown hair, full lips, regular teeth, a smile that made her cheeks dimple. A bit bossy, too, but then, so he thought, every woman has her faults. "You won't get to first base with this straight-laced girl," his classmates told him, yet they threw him envious glances whenever they saw the two of them together. Date followed date, brightening his senior year, pushing his dreams of Asia or Africa on the back-burner. And then they both drank too much at the hospital's Christmas party. It turned out that she wasn't as straight-laced as her reputation; nor was he as cautious as a future doctor should have been. When she told him the news a few weeks later, he proposed marriage and she said yes. Their daughter, whom they named Mary, added to the worldwide population explosion three months after her father's graduation.

Internship in Philadelphia. Alfred, always deeply concerned about the patients under his care, worked harder than his fellow interns, often returning to the hospital late in the evening to recheck a seriously ill man or woman. Domestic discord began to overshadow marital bliss.

"After dinner I must go back to the hospital to review my charts. We have a conference tomorrow morning. I'm also worried about the man on two East with endocarditis."

"But it's your night off. Stay home with your family. Don't Mary and I count for anything? Let whoever is on duty worry about the sick man."

Toward the end of his internship his long-submerged wish to go to an underdeveloped country surfaced again. As expected, Becky sneered at the idea.

"You're a family man now; your wife and daughter come first. I'm not going to live in some flea-bitten country in the tropics. And I want Mary to grow up here in the United States. You better decide where you're going to practice."

He himself harbored misgivings about his ability to handle the huge patient load in a tropical country, compulsively thorough as he was, spending at least half an hour with each new patient, whether it was headaches, a sore throat or depression. After much soul-searching he decided to become a general practitioner. In San Manuel an old G.P., about to retire, was looking for a young doctor to take over his practice. Alfred grabbed this opportunity; yet he never forgot his dream about the tropics. Nor did he forget his hope for a son, whom Becky failed to bear. She lost her second pregnancy at three months and never again became pregnant. When Mary was four, her parents adopted a Korean boy.

How much fun his practice had been in those early years! Every week brought new, exciting cases. At home Alfred gladly took over more than his share of raising the children, thus giving Becky's outside activities free reign. She was tireless: golf, bridge, garden club, ladies' auxiliary, hints of political ambition.

Gradually things began to change. During the past decade a spate of freshly-baked specialists had descended upon San Manuel like a swarm of locusts, virtually monopolizing all cases within their respective fields, reducing the general practitioner to a doctor for common, minor ailments. Five years ago, after a bitter staff fight, the new doctors succeeded in having the hospital's bylaws amended, so that a family practitioner no longer could deliver a baby there, nor perform even minor surgery, nor take charge of any case in the intensive care unit.

"How was your day at the office?" Becky asked.

"Twenty-five patients, mostly colds, sore throats, school physicals; a few hypochondriacs. I wish I was practicing somewhere where I could do all I've been trained for."

"Here you go again! Never satisfied; unhappy because one day you haven't had an interesting case. How many other doctors see twenty-five patients in one day? Be happy! Count your blessings!" And she enumerated, for the hundredth time, his seven reasons for mandatory happiness:

"Good health; a loving wife; Mary; Kim; your profession; our home; last, but not least, money."

Right after dinner she rushed off to a board meeting of the ladies' auxiliary. Mary went out on a date; Kim left for basketball practice. Alfred, alone, leafed through a few medical journals, then buried his head in the latest issue of *Option*, a publication listing medical opportunities in areas of need.

He began to hate his practice, shun friends, lose interest in his home and family. Depression! Becky couldn't understand it; his moodiness enraged her. Bitter domestic quarrels ensued; there were talks of divorce, and finally a month-long separation. Gradually the medication prescribed by his psychiatrist brightened his mood. An emotional reconciliation followed.

"Dr. Rubin wants me to take a long vacation."

"We have never had a real honeymoon; let's take one now, far away."

The next day the usual paper blizzard descending on his desk contained a glossy travel folder advertising a three weeks' trip to South America. Photographs of Spanish-style baroque churches, colorful Indian markets, Inca ruins, luxury hotels, night clubs, and bikini-clad bathing beauties filled its pages, tempting the reader to invest several thousand dollars in "the adventure of a lifetime." That's why they were here now, on the train from Machupicchu, the trip's "crowning jewel," back to Cusco, with one more day remaining before their return flight to the U.S.

Suddenly people rushed to the windows; admiring exclamations resounded through the railroad car. Hundreds of feet below, in the center of a sea of lights that extended glittering fingers up the surrounding hills, there stood the great cathedral of Cusco, aglow in floodlight like a mountaintop at sunset. Alfred awakened his wife who joined in the multilingual chorus of admiration, then duly recorded the event in her travel diary. One hour later they reached their hotel.

The final day's schedule called for the visits of two museums in Cusco, plus an excursion to the ruins of Pisaq. More ancient stones and artifacts, more hordes of camera-toting tourists, Alfred thought. Feigning a severe headache, he refused to go along next morning. After Becky and the others had left, he hired a cab and told the driver, who understood English, to take him to some Quechua Indian villages.

They all looked similar: one-story, thick-walled houses with roofs of thatch or curved tile; a few eucalyptus trees; llamas or similar animals grazing in the fields; impassive-looking women in long black skirts, wearing broad-brimmed, colorful hats; lean, muscular men, their faces the color of tanned leather; boys and girls, intelligence and curiosity sparkling in their black eyes. Alfred talked with some of them, loosening their tongues with money and using his driver, Antonio, a Quechua himself, as interpreter.

The dirt road wound through a canyon and over barren hills to a remote village, Antonio's birthplace, where the driver invited his fare into his parents' house. After due introduction Antonio's father asked the *medico norteamericano* to examine his fourteen-year-old daughter, who was *muy enferma* (very sick). Alfred, not licensed in Peru, and not carrying any medical equipment other than a thermometer, complied reluctantly.

High fever, vomiting, a rigid neck: MENINGITIS! Josefa was

desperately ill. It took all of Alfred's power of persuasion, plus Antonio's help, to convince her parents of the urgent need to send her to the hospital in Cusco, two hours away. There followed a hectic ride, Antonio taking the curves like a madman, in spite of Alfred's plea for caution, with the patient lying on the backseat, her mother crouching next to her. The ancient cab reeked of vomitus! In Cusco, Josefa was admitted immediately to the Hospital Regional; the young Peruvian physician who took over the case impressed Alfred as capable and dedicated. Alfred himself stayed at the hospital till a spinal tap had confirmed his diagnosis; then he said good-bye and for an hour, in deep thought, wandered aimlessly all over the ancient Inca capital, through narrow streets and over wide plazas. How long since he had seen the last case of meningitis in his own practice? At least five years. Today, for the first time in many months, he experienced the glowing sense of pride and self-fulfillment of a healer. When he returned to the hospital, Josefa had stopped vomiting; an intravenous infusion with a massive dose of Penicillin was running into her arm. She had a better than even chance of recovery.

At the hotel while waiting for dinner, Becky, with reproachful enthusiasm, recounted to Alfred the many things she had seen and he had missed. The last entry in her diary read: "Begging children everywhere; I'm sick of them; glad we're leaving for home tomorrow."

"And how did you spend the day?" she asked. He told her.

"So that's what you did instead of coming along with the rest of the group! You said you had a headache. All the ruins and museums you missed. That's what you paid for, didn't you?"

"I saved a life. That's my calling, isn't it? But for me that Indian girl would have died."

Becky shrugged her shoulders but didn't answer; he could guess her thoughts. After dinner he wrote a letter, sealed and stamped it, and slipped it into his coat pocket.

Late that night they returned to the hotel from a gaudy

farewell party. Becky, a little tipsy, sank into an armchair in the empty lobby, pulled her diary from her handbag, and rattled off the names of the places they had visited in Peru: "Lima, Arequipa, Juliaca, Ruins of Silustani, Puno, Lake Titicaca, Island of Taquil, Cusco, Machupicchu, Market of Chincheros, Ruins of Pisaq."

Alfred, also with a few drinks under his belt, was pacing the lobby. Journey's end; their suitcases were packed, the plane would leave at ten the next morning. Back to his stale medical practice, to medical journals describing diseases he would never see, hospital procedures he would never be permitted to carry out himself. Back to dull staff meetings and ritual golf games; back to his role of a tolerated bystander at his wife's social functions and his daughter's parties, important to his family mainly as the source of the fuel that made the engine run.

Suddenly Becky, leafing through her diary, interrupted his thoughts.

"Alfred, do you remember what our guide at Machupicchu told us the sacred number seven stands for? I forgot."

"For the blessings I'm supposed to count every day," he snapped back. "Don't enumerate them, I know them by heart. Damn it, I want to work at a place where they really need me and where I'm permitted to do everything I've been trained for, without having to refer each challenging problem to some specialist who doesn't know half as much medicine as I do; I want to work some place where I can save lives every day."

"Nonsense!" she shouted, making the sleepy clerk at the desk perk up in surprise. "You're never satisfied with what you have. Here we've just spent three wonderful weeks in South America. Think of all the beautiful places we've visited and all the interesting things we've seen. And still you're not happy. We went on this trip to patch up our marriage. I'm sick and tired of your brooding; if you keep it up I'll get a divorce."

Alfred looked straight into his wife's eyes. "All right," he said calmly, "no more brooding. I've come to a decision. I'll accept a one year's appointment as physician-in-chief at the Brotherhood Hospital in Opobo, Nigeria. The position was listed in the latest issue of *Option*. I wrote my letter of acceptance this evening but wasn't sure whether I should mail it. I'm going to mail it now."

"You wouldn't do that to me!" Becky yelled. Alfred pulled the letter from his coat pocket. Becky jumped up and tried to grab it, but alcohol had distorted her coordination. She staggered, barely regained her balance, and collapsed back into the armchair, shouting, "Alfred, don't mail this damned letter!"

He walked over to the reception desk, dropped the letter into the mail slot, then returned to his wife, sat down next to her, and put his arm around her shoulders. To his surprise, she didn't push him away.

Born in Vienna, Dr. Gerhart A. Drucker emigrated to the USA in 1936. He practiced medicine from 1941 to 1982 when he retired to devote more time to his lifelong hobby writing prose and poetry. He is now preparing his fourth volume of poetry; he has published short stories in journals as diverse as Skiing *and* Medical Economics. *Dr. Drucker is fluent in English, German and French.*

"Alexei knew, or rather he felt, that there was something wrong with Tamara's reasoning, but it was pleasant to think yourself more important than you were in reality."

The Present Day

SERGEI YESIN

THEY wouldn't let her into the ward to see him.

Tamara was so upset that she gasped for breath, she pressed her slim fingers to her breast and felt her heart pounding hollowly beneath the thin material of her blouse.

Yes, it was the end of everything, she was losing everything at once: if the rumor got around that Alexei had had a heart attack, it would be the end of his career; when the time came for the next promotion, someone would be bound to remember his heart attack and say that Alexei would be taking it easy now, and that meant the end of the road, he had no future left. And he was only forty years old. And then again she realized that they didn't have so much left ahead of them. She didn't waste time moping. What if they hadn't let her into the ward? There was no way she could help her husband at the moment, anyway. She wouldn't behave like the other idiot wives and hang about outside the door, she would act, with no panic or confusion. Life had dealt her enough blows, she was well trained. She had to act, and then they would see who came out on top. First she had to put on her face and tidy herself up, and then set to work.

Nurses were constantly flitting up and down the corridor on nimble legs. Their white coats were all short, they wore starched caps, their eyes were all made up, they had fashionable shoes on their feet—no, no, Tamara was not to be fooled, this carelessness with the fashionable shoes wasn't some naturally acquired habit; the nurses probably arrived at the hospital in worn old boots and when they got here they blew a few specks of dust from their shiny shoes and took in every little crack with a quick glance, before carefully putting them on in order to clatter along the corridor with an emphatically casual air. But now was not the time for Tamara to be irritated by their youth, nor for her to provoke them with her elegant bearing, her Parisian perfumes and her Italian shoes. They would be useful to her, these little nymphs, they would be useful to Alexei, to her future.

Tamara stooped slightly and drew the white visitor's coat more tightly around her to conceal the flared denim skirt with the slit— the very height of fashion—and went over to the window. It was time to do her face. She turned away slightly—from her back one might get the impression that she was prostrated with grief—took her compact out of her handbag, and before she powdered her cheeks with the puff, she examined her face carefully. She studied it with the tenacious, fixed expression of a general observing the field of battle from beneath his raised hand. And then—to work! First the forehead and the cheeks, shake the excess powder from the nose, outline eyebrows. Everything seemed to be in order now. She wouldn't call herself beautiful. Her nose turned up too much, her skin was a bit dry, she had wrinkles under her eyes, and a little bit of fat had even begun to gather beneath her chin, but there was something about her eyes, with their dry, piercing glitter. Like a singer sounding a brief note, without opening her lips. As she observed her face in the little mirror, Tamara cleared her throat. Her weapon was in order, and she knew how to proceed.

What feeble men she always ended up with! Why was it always these milksops that life exalted? They let themselves be overwhelmed by their emotions, and this was the result—poor Alexei! Everything was just beginning to come together so well—and then this heart attack! Why was it that she who could see right through anyone, who understood every subtle shift in the feelings of anyone she was talking to, who knew when to say nothing and when to speak, why was it that she, Tamara, could not keep a grip on anything? And once again she pulled herself up short: the main thing was not to let it get to you, not to weaken.

As she went down the stairs, Tamara was feverishly thinking where she should phone from. They would let her use the phone in the interns' room, she could phone from the head doctor's office—he was bound to have an office; but there might be somebody in there, and she didn't need any witnesses. It would take too long to get home: Alexei had been brought here from work, they were worried at the office, they might beat her to it and start inquiring at the hospital. Although it was cold and wet outside, it would propably be best if she rang from a public phone.

Tamara ran across the hospital yard and dashed towards a telephone booth. Her legs were soaked and chilled, but as she dialed the number, she tried not to think of her own discomfort—her voice had to sound bright and natural. The phone was answered immediately by the secretary in reception.

"Galya, this is Tamara."

"I'm so glad you've rung, Tamara. We're all very worried. How's Alexei, how's he feeling?"

"It's nothing to worry about, Galochka," Tamara switched on her very warmest intonation, "nothing to worry about. Just a simple stenocardia. At forty,"—by speaking confidentially with his secretary about his age, Tamara sought to win her over as an ally, but she deliberately took two years off her husband's age: of course everyone knew which year he was born, but let them all think of him as younger, more reliable, with his future before him. "At forty it's perfectly normal: he had a bit of stress, caught a cold and had a mild attack, it will all be fine soon."

"Alexei must take a good rest," Galochka stated reasonably.

"Of course, of course. You're absolutely right, dear. That's very good thinking." Tamara flattered the secretary in passing. "He must take a good rest."

"There can be all kinds of complications," Galochka went on.

"Exactly," Tamara concluded one theme, and as she went on to the next, the most important one, she changed the tone of her voice slightly. It became more resonant, more insinuating and significant. Galya herself clearly realized that this dress-parade voice was not intended for her.

"You probably want to talk to Yuri Sergeyevich?" she asked.

"I've already spoken to you," Tamara replied evasively. "Do I need to talk to him too?"

"Oh, you must! Yuri Sergeyevich is worried."

"Well, in that case, please ask him to pick up his phone."

Now she had to face another skirmish with destiny.

It was cold and damp in the telephone booth. Through the glass, streaked with rain, she could see the cheerless facade of the hospital and part of the yard. Two female orderlies, shielding themselves from the rain under pieces of polythene sheeting, were carrying baskets of rubbish to the dump. It was good weather for sitting in a warm room and gazing out of the window.

In the cold telephone receiver she could hear distant rustlings—that was Galochka setting off from her corner across the room to Yuri Sergeyevich's office. Tamara could picture the reception office—familiar, warm and comfortable. A color television, a soft carpet, a small electric samovar always on the boil on the broad window sill, Galochka's desk, cluttered with half a dozen telephones, and two doors—behind one was Alexei's office, and behind the other the office of his boss, Yuri Sergeyevich. Alexei's office would be empty for a long time now.

She loved to call in to see her husband in the middle of the working day. In Alexei's office she was always fascinated by the switches, the noiseless American telex, the loudspeakers, the telephones—the accoutrements of the intensive work of a top boss; she was fascinated and delighted by all these electrical and electronic devices, which not only assisted Alexei by supplying instantaneous information and transforming his words into commands, orders and instructions, but made his position and his power particularly obvious to any visitor. This was the office that was to have created

Alexei's future, which Tamara had already constructed in her head. And Alexei was so very close to achieving this goal. After all wasn't his position as assistant director the springboard to independent work abroad? Sitting beside these devices and telexes, wouldn't Alexei have been able to choose the country and even the place to match his own and Tamara's personal preference? Hadn't Ivan, Alexei's college friend, that fat oaf, whose place Alexei now occupied, gone off to West Germany for three years? That dozy hog with his cackling wife Sonya and his three fat daughters was strolling around Bonn now and riding in a Mercedes. What made him any better than Alexei? Alexei knew the language better, probably better than anyone in the Ministry, it was no accident that Ivan himself, and even Yuri Sergeyevich, a member of the Ministry's Board, didn't call in a staff translator for tricky negotiations, but Alexei. Not only was he a marvelous simultaneous translator, but he handled himself well, he knew about industry, he knew the market situation. And now this idiotic, this stupid heart attack!

There was a rustling in the receiver. Then Tamara could clearly hear Galochka pick up the phone and say in her official, slightly strained voice:

"Tamara, I'm putting you through to Yuri Sergeyevich."

The orderlies, shielded from the rain by polythene sheets, were returning to the hospital, chattering happily as they walked. The rain became heavier. Once again Tamara quickly ran her eyes over the facade of the hospital, gray in patches from the rain. Then Tamara glanced quickly at her blue Zhiguli car—the export model—huddling by the main entrance, and prepared herself for the next skirmish. The stereotype was called "The Loving Wife, alarmed, perhaps excessively so, by her husband's state of health."

"Hello, Tamara," Yuri Sergeyevich's velvety baritone sounded in the earpiece, "How is Alexei? I was with the chief when he was taken ill. I hope it's not too serious?"

"Thank you, Yuri Sergeyevich," Tamara launched into her subtle act—"I phoned you,"—she tried to pronounce the word "you" so that he would detect the special weight she gave to it—"I phoned you to tell you not to worry." It was a good move to bind Yuri Sergeyevich with her affected concern and involve him in Alexei's fate.

"Not at all, Tamara, it's my duty."

"A duty which, unfortunately, not everyone fulfills nowadays."
There was a tearful trembling in Tamara's voice.

"What exactly is wrong with Alexei?"

Tamara employed the same term that she had used already in
the conversation with Galochka:

"Stenocardia, and he probably caught a cold as well; one thing
on top of another. I don't think he'll be in bed for too long, Alexei
is strong."

"Be sure to keep me informed."

"Of course. Lord, what a blow!" Tamara blurted out.

"It could happen to anyone," mumbled Yuri Sergeyevich in a
softer voice. "You keep a grip on yourself and don't weaken. Call
if you need any help."

"Thank you, Yuri Sergeyevich, my best wishes to you and your
wife. Take care of yourself..."

There was a rapid beeping in the receiver. Tamara ran to her
car, remembering as she did so that in all the bustle she had
forgotten to remove the windshield wipers. The way people are
nowadays, she thought, you only have to blink and the wipers are
gone...

That was her second success of the day—after her conversation
with Yuri Sergeyevich—the wipers were still in place. Tamara
opened the car door, carefully warmed up the engine, and with a
final glance at the hospital entrance, she engaged the clutch.
Driving calmed her a little. It wasn't the first misfortune she'd had
to cope with. Her husband was in good hands, she'd get him on his
feet using the accelerated method, then get him into a sanatorium,
it was a good thing Alexei had not used his leave from last year;
then in to work for one day—they wouldn't let you take two sets of
leave together—and back to the sanatorium, for this year's leave.
She'd find the right "personal" reasons for taking one leave straight
after the other. No one would be able to unearth the real reasons.

Tamara confidently shifted gear and as she turned on to another
street she glimpsed the hospital through the rear window in her
mirror. How was Alexei? He was a strong man, he wouldn't let her

down, he'd pull through. Her place now was not beside him, her place was by the telephone.

When he came round, Alexei was not tormented by not knowing where he was. The sudden, unbearable pain behind his breastbone, the attempt to reach the bell button with his finger, the frightened face of his secretary Galochka when she ran in, the doctor's white coat, even the preliminary diagnosis whispered so that he wouldn't hear it—"Looks like infarction"—he could remember it all clearly.

Alexei opened his eyes and immediately met the gaze of a young nurse. There was a momentary gleam of satisfaction in her eyes.

"How are you feeling?"

"Fine," answered Alexei.

"No pain anywhere?"

"Not so far."

The nurse was looking at him keenly and mistrustfully, as though she suspected him of concealing some important secret out of excessive bravado.

With a hand that was slightly rough from constant washing, she took his wrist and began to concentrate. Her face with the plucked eyebrows and skillfully applied make-up was almost funny, it was too youthful. The doll's mask contradicted her seriousness. There was something about the behavior of the tiny vein pulsing on Alexei's wrist that the nurse did not like. But she clearly decided not to allow the patient to feel her concern. She carefully set down Alexei's hand and said:

"My name's Anna."

"Mine's Alexei, and I would like to have met you under different circumstances."

Anna did not acknowledge the joke, she only gave a polite half-smile, but her brows remained knitted in concern. Things are not too good, thought Alexei.

"Would you like me to call the orderly? You won't be able to get out of bed for a while now."

"I know," said Alexei.

"I'm glad you do," the nurse cut in sharply. "That will make things easier for you and for me. Shall I call the orderly now?"

"I don't need anything for the moment," answered Alexei.

"I'm going out for a short while," said Anna.

"For the doctor?"

"Yes. But don't you worry." It was clear from her expression that she was angry at not having been able to conceal her concern. "If you feel poorly, press the button on the wall. If you want, you can breathe some oxygen, the mask is on your pillow. Do you understand?"

"I'm very bright," joked Alexei.

Anna smiled, and was clearly very annoyed that she had violated the distance between herself and the patient.

When she went out, Alexei thought again. Things look bad. It could be curtains if I'm not careful. And an old thought that had already been haunting him before filtered implacably into his consciousness: They've driven me into a corner. If not this time, then the next, I'm done for. Ivan was right. But it's strange that this (out of some inexplicable superstition Alexei immediately began to refer to his illness as "this") should have happened today, when everything began so calmly and well. Perhaps it was the weather?

The night before he had gone to bed early and quickly fallen asleep. His sleep had been light, without any dreams or thoughts of work. He had woken of his own accord, without the alarm clock, and as usual Tamara was already up, and there was a pleasant smell of breakfast in the flat. First of all Tamara gave him grated apple to eat—she claimed that it was good for the stomach and for the heart. And once again Alexei had been astonished by Tamara's energy and the fact that after almost three years of marriage her enthusiastic and tender attentions continued unabated. As though she still had to win him, to flatter him with comfort. Then Alexei had eaten some cottage cheese pancakes—the way he liked them with hardly any flour—and drunk a cup of coffee while he read the newspaper.. Before he was even awake Tamara had gone down in the lift to get the mail from the box. And at exactly twenty to nine Tamara had said, "Time to go."

"Maybe you'll go with me today?" asked Alexei. "Why should you be bothered driving?"

"No. That's your official car, not mine. The drivers are always gossiping, and I don't want them saying at the office that you drive your wife to work in an office car. Your reputation must be above reproach."

That was his final conversation with his wife and his final unpressured moment of the day, although Alexei definitely remembered that the day had been calmer than the ones before it. In fact, during the last two years days like it had been very rare.

As he sat in the car, on the left hand side in the back—that looked more respectable, it was safer, and all the chiefs sat there, Tamara said—Alexei thought about the corrections to the quarterly plan, then he decided that today he would tell Tsyganov that it was time for him to retire, although Tsyganov clearly did not want to. They already had an obliging and energetic youngster to replace Tsyganov, and he would certainly get things moving, but no sooner did Alexei think that he would have to tell Tsyganov, an old man burdened with a family, that his working style and methods did not suit either Alexei as the boss, or the staff of the department, than he immediately began to feel awkward in his comfortable car. He imagined the hunted expression in Tsyganov's eyes, and the ruses Tsyganov would resort to. And then there would be the complaint to the trade union committee and the Party committee; he would have to go round them all to prove his case, and say the truthful but harsh and hurtful words to Tsyganov's face. And there was the inter-departmental conference today—once again the struggle to stir people into action. Of course, it would be easier for him too if he could simply work in the same old way, dealing with the same old clients, the same old reliable firms they had done business with for years. But times moved on. They had to look for new opportunities, new clients, new intermediaries. And they couldn't afford to miss anything. A quotation carelessly overlooked in the morning could mean losses incurred in the negotiations that evening. And then there was the constant smoking during business conferences and those little glasses of cognac which not only had to be raised while you gazed meaningfully into your partner's eyes, but occasionally drunk as well. For that you needed Ivan's iron constitution, his sensibly harsh attitude towards yourself. Perhaps Ivan was right after all when he said, "Alexei, you deserve this job, you are my friend and I have to recommend you. But think it over again. So far you've always had my protection at work. But now you're putting the yoke on your own neck. Can you handle it?" At the time, from the outside, Ivan's work and his problems had seemed less complicated to Alexei...Ivan had said, "You're volunteering for hard labor." And it had always seemed to him that Ivan did almost nothing. He toyed with his papers, smiled as he sought the simple and apparently commonplace words to convince people that they had made the wrong decision, and even when he refused their requests, everyone left Ivan's office happy and satisfied. And Tamara had said, "You mustn't refuse the job. If you must know, although I respect him a great deal, Ivan is only so well in with the boss because you work for him. It's all set up for him. That's why he's able to smile and hobnob with the boss, and go on trips abroad, and leave everything up to you for so long. He takes advantage of your friendship."

Alexei knew, or rather he felt, that there was something wrong with Tamara's reasoning, but it was pleasant to think yourself more important than you were in reality; he didn't argue. And then it became clear—and so far he was the only one to realize this—that being a good head of department in a firm was quite a different matter from managing all the ongoing work of that firm. And he could sense that soon other people would realize it too. And Alexei knew what a terrible thing this would be. So now he had no freedom at all in his relations with his colleagues. He was the boss, the manager—and he was afraid of every next meeting with his subordinates. He worked out in advance the phrases he was going to use in conversations and discussions. He became tense and more formal than he should be. Alexei was aware that in his work he relied less on the strength of his own personality than on the authority of his impressive position, the authority of the chair that Ivan had occupied.

He kept himself going by sheer will power. He was already sick of it all—the thousand different jobs he had to deal with, the concern for his own prestige, and his wife's need for amusement and attention. He'd like to dump it all. Tell the boss straight out: I want to go back to my own job, that I know and I can do properly.

But for the time being he would carry on toiling away. Secretly, Alexei half-believed that it was all the result of lack of experience. Any time now he would learn something new, he would discover some new knack, he would pick up the ends of the threads and sniff out the mysterious secret of his trade, which Ivan had perhaps concealed from him. He would survive the crisis of the avalanche of work that had overwhelmed him, and then he would make it. Just as happy and successful and efficient as Ivan. At the same time Alexei realized that he lacked something which Ivan had, he didn't have the right kind of strength, maybe he just didn't have the spark that was required, the fire in the blood, maybe he just didn't have the talent?

That day even the daily morning review session had gone more easily than ever before.

These sessions usually aroused the same images in Alexei's mind: a circus and an animal tamer who goes out into the ring, into a cage where the tigers are already waiting. The tigers rush about over the sawdust, waving their tails to and fro and frightening each other with their roaring and their gaping pink jaws. And he, the animal tamer, has to subjugate them all to his will. First of all these big, fierce cats have to sit on their pedestals. They don't want to do this although, of course, they know that come what may they will take their places and then go through their paces in reluctant fury. A blow here, and a raised whip there, a shout or a hard stare here and a pat on the soft fur there—and at last they're all in their places. The tamer's back is soaking wet, the embroidered shirt is glued by sweat to the bare body beneath it, but he knows the show must go on, the public has paid its money, and he has to get on with the job, and his tigers, lions, panthers and pumas in mini-skirts must swing on the swings, jump through the blazing hoop and lie at his feet like some great patterned carpet (he knows how much this stinking carpet hates him and is ever ready to rise up roaring on its hind legs and start a brawl), they must walk the tightrope and perform at his command all the tricks that have been practiced beforehand, and he has to force his tigers to do what he has planned for them to do, otherwise the next day's show will be still more difficult, or maybe even quite impossible to manage. And tomorrow—the same thing over again: physical and mental strain of every fiber, gaping jaws and beasts reluctantly running through their paces...

While the heads of departments, weighed down with reports and other papers, came into his office and took their places—some at the conference table, others in their favorite corners—the usual images rose up in Alexei's memory, but this meeting went off more easily than usual. Judging from the reports, things were going well in the trade representations abroad: yesterday, as the formula goes, mutually advantageous deals were signed with the firms targeted, for once the opinions of the department heads coincided with Alexei's, and even Tsyganov had everything all tied down. Tsyganov didn't answer him in his usual derisive tone, which implied that Alexei's questions were absolutely stupid and naive, and Tsyganov was only answering them because Alexei, this youngster whom blind fortune had raised up on the crest of its administrative wave, was his boss, and Tsyganov's old retainer's ethics would not allow him to insult his boss and show everyone else how frivolous and incompetent he was as a manager. No, this time Tsyganov had been remarkably deferential in agreeing with Alexei's arguments and his plan for conducting negotiations with Herr Friedmann from West Germany, a real expert and owner of an intermediary firm. Tsyganov even seemed genuinely pleased with Alexei's idea, and surprised everyone by not simply accepting it, as the proper thing to do, something he had already thought out anyway, but by actually admitting that "he hadn't thought of that." And then Alexei began to wonder whether he ought to force Tsyganov to retire. He didn't seem such a reactionary after all, and if sometimes someone couldn't come up with a new idea, then the boss was not there just to filter other people's ideas, but to think them up himself.

After the daily session Alexei had glanced through the newspapers in which Galochka had already marked certain articles for his attention, carefully read the telegrams and telexes that had come in during the night, noted down a plan for the day and a list of urgent matters on a sheet of paper, and having phoned Yuri Sergeyevich to say he was on his way, had walked across the reception office to make his report.

Yuri Sergeyevich was seated as usual at his huge desk absolutely empty of papers, drinking tea with milk. He was heavy, fat, and thought that tea with milk would help him lose weight, or at least keep his weight within reasonable limits. Today even Yuri Sergeyevich's mood was tolerable, almost equable, but Alexei was nervous, just as he always was when he entered this office, as he used to be in Ivan's time when on rare occasions—once or twice a year—Yuri Sergeyevich drew him out of the crowded warren of the ministry's offices.

Yuri Sergeyevich also received the report relatively calmly. He immediately asked Alexei to take a seat, which was a good sign in itself, and quickly signed all Alexei's papers one after the other. Alexei, whose desk was literally piled high with files, inquiry notes and documents (before signing anything or even visaing it he always left it to sit for a while), was always astonished at the speed with which Yuri Sergeyevich dispatched any piece of paper from his desk—assigning it for action either by Alexei or one of his other subordinates. It was a smooth and faultless style of work. Maybe it was precisely because Alexei had not fully mustered it that he was in such a sorry state now? He agonized over every piece of paper that hadn't been signed yet, was frequently dissatisfied with the way things were worded, and took documents home, but the most important thing was that all these unsettled matters stuck in his mind. He was unable to extricate himself from his administrative whirlpool. Visiting friends or dining at home, in the car, everywhere and always, out the weekend, day and night, he felt as though he was at work, bogged down in the hustle and bustle of current business, which now, here in hospital, he realized was not all that important. Alexei didn't trust anyone, he snatched at everything himself, he worried and panicked and was afraid of making a mistake. Ivan was not like that. Of course, it had been much easier for Ivan. And now Alexei realized that as soon as his old friends, his fellow-employees with whom he used to drink tea in the canteen and play chess after work, had realized that he was trying to grasp everything and check everything himself—they had immediately dumped all their papers on him. And they had taken pleasure in watching—he had not disappointed them—as Alexei floundered in this paper sea, sinking ever deeper, and then they had stopped thinking and making independent decisions, heaping all the work on to him. There you go, Alexei, carry that lot. Ivan had been proved right—he was not up to carrying this onerous burden—and now the burden had crushed him.

By the end of the meeting Yuri Sergeyevich was in a really good mood, he had dealt with practically all the current business of the day. He asked Galochka for another cup of tea with milk, and while his secretary went down to the canteen, while he drank his tea in a leisurely fashion, he indulged himself by telling Alexei about his grandchildren, savoring his own words as he spoke. Of course, they were the sweetest and most talented children of their age in the world—Alexei had already accepted that, but he knew that in a few minutes Tokyo would be calling him, and Galochka would not dare to interrupt their conversation, and straight after that there would be the meeting with the experts who were probably already gathering in the conference hall. If Alexei sat there calmly for another ten minutes appearing to be interested in this sentimental old man's twaddle, the whole day would be shot to hell. Like railway wagons during an accident, the conferences and business meetings would pile up on each other, and finally, Alexei's day, overwhelmed by the weight of unrealized plans, would collapse, and then the personal plans of dozens, or hundreds of people would be thrown out of joint.

These unnecessary "lyrical" half-hours with Yuri Sergeyevich were his most difficult times. He had to smile sincerely at the pranks of the smart grandchildren, and keep up the conversation as though he were profoundly interested, while all the time his brain was working overtime as he conjured up dozens of formulas for apologies and deducted the minutes he had lost from the essential meetings, the telephone calls and the time for analyzing events and discussions. He began to feel a heavy weariness in his forearms and his hands, but still he didn't have the strength, or perhaps the diplomatic skill, politely but firmly to put an end to the conversation.

Finally, almost an hour later, when he had drunk another glass of tea, which Galochka had once again fetched from the canteen on the third floor, Yuri Sergeyevich let Alexei go. Alexei's shirt was already soaking wet, his plans for the day were in shreds, but as it turned out he had been worrying too much and things were not really in such bad shape. In the reception office, as Alexei crossed from Yuri Sergeyevich's office to his own, Galochka warned him: first, Tokyo was asking for their conversation to be postponed until tomorrow; second, the experts were tired of waiting for him and Tsyganov had started the meeting on his own initiative; third, Galochka reminded Alexei that in an hour he had to be at the Council of Ministers, and she knew from experience that if Alexei didn't take lunch immediately, then he would go hungry all day, and so she had taken the liberty of ordering lunch to be brought to his office. Alexei was about to flare up and object that in that hour he could have resolved, or at least begun, a multitude of little matters, but he suddenly thought that Galochka was probably right, his health came first, and waved his hand and said with a smile, "Okay, Galochka, bring in the lunch."

At the very moment when Alexei was finishing his favorite compote of tinned pears, he began to feel ill. An unbearable pain erupted in his chest. He put the unfinished glass of compote to one side and went on sitting there in his revolving chair, streaming with cold sweat. A thought flashed through his mind: The first signal of age, and then another, a reassuring one: It will pass in a moment, I'll wait for the pain to pass and then set off...But the pain did not pass. Sweat coated his eyes and dripped down behind his collar. His secretary's experience saved him: without bothering to ask any questions, Galochka called the emergency service. The only thing he wouldn't allow them to do was to put him on the stretcher in his office. He went down in the lift, leaning on the doctor, walked out through the hallway, past the policeman at the entrance, got into the ambulance and lay down immediately. They carried him into the hospital.

Anyway, I'm glad it's not a stroke, Alexei thought when the nurse's heels clattered in the corridor outside the ward. A stroke means you lose your memory. But this is only painful; the motor might be broken, but that's not the most important thing in a man, not the electronics, not the brain...

Anna came in first, followed by two technicians in white coats who wheeled in a massive piece of equipment gleaming with nickel and switches of various colors. They were followed by a relatively young woman with a stethoscope round her neck—the doctor.

"Don't be afraid," said Anna, taking the initiative. "This is a diagnostic apparatus. It won't hurt. And a fine piece of equipment it is!" There was a note of pride in her voice. "The only one in the country!"

"There's certainly nothing to be afraid of." The doctor gently and patiently took Alexei's wrist and began to concentrate.

"It's not too bad, is it, doctor?" asked Alexei.

"Of course it's not too bad, but the repairs will take a little time."

"I'll be your very best patient: I'll lie on my back and not move a muscle."

"The new methods don't require that, but you must only turn over with the nurse's help."

"You mean it was an infarction?"

"A very severe stenocardia," the doctor said with a faint smile. "You'll have to talk less and save your strength."

"I told him the same thing," said Anna. Then she joked, "If you talk, we'll discharge you."

Meanwhile the technicians had untangled the wires and with Anna's assistance they set about fixing the sensors to Alexei's body. The rubber suckers felt cool on his skin, and the fact that so many people were working to preserve his health made him feel certain that everything would be all right. And although he was ill, and lying on his back, and they wouldn't allow him to move a muscle, and probably not even read for the time being, he could still think! In this pause, this period for which sickness had isolated him from the vain bustle of his daily cares, he would analyze his mistakes thoroughly, weigh everything up, and his career be damned, life was more precious!—he would finally make up his mind...But then, would Tamara agree with him? She'd probably try to persuade him into it again, and she would, and he'd put back on his administrative yoke.

"There's no doubt at all that you'll come through all right," the doctor interrupted Alexei's train of thought. She had already finished her examination, having glanced at the ribbons of the printers, and then listened long and carefully to Alexei's chest. "Anyway, we'll consult about you tomorrow."

The technicians had already wound up their wires and were carefully dragging the trolley into the corridor.

"At first try to lie on your back. Don't worry, and sleep as much as you can..."

"What about reading?"

"No reading."

"Can I think?"

The doctor caught his irony.

"Not so that you tire yourself. And try to talk as little as possible."

"I'll try."

"Has the pain gone?"

"My heart doesn't hurt."

"That's good. Good night. If you can't sleep, or you feel unwell, ring the bell. Anna will come and give an injection."

In actual fact, Alexei knew all there was to know about his illness: there were so many stories in their institutional milieu about heart attacks, the kinds of pain, the system of treatment—told, of course, from first-hand experience; these stories came in the canteen in the course of low-fat, high-vitamin lunches. It was a manager's disease, and these managers knew all there was to know about their illness, they had it off as pat as any doctor. So the artificially cheerful conversation with the doctor was of no interest to Alexei, after all it was their concern, not his, to pull him through—all he had to do was to save his energy, lie on his back, sleep and eat. Alexei closed his eyes, and the medical team began to hurry about their business.

The doctor whispered a few more instructions to Anna, there was a rustling as she walked across the room and then the sound of the door being closed. Then Anna went quietly over to the door. Through eyes open just a slit Alexei saw Anna stand there for a moment, listening for the footsteps in the corridor to die away, then stick her head round the door, turning it to look both ways, and immediately slip out of the ward, carefully pulling the door handle behind her. And then immediately there was whispering and quiet male laughter outside. Alexei chuckled to himself: Hospital romances...Only natural for a young girl! Who might the lucky man be? And his thoughts skipped on to a different subject: What is Hecuba to me? ...Laughter, muffled whisperings and bustlings on the other side of the wall...The events of the day came back to his mind—the work that had been done, Yuri Sergeyevich with his glass of tea; then Ivan appeared, and his happy smile, almost childish in its excess of mischief, Tamara's face flashed before him, and then—maybe he really had dozed off—the face of Lydia, his former wife. Lydia looked into his eyes as she had during their last meeting on Pushkin Square, the day before Alexei was appointed to Ivan's job, and said, "That woman will be the death of you!" What had Tamara got to do with it, Alexei wondered yet again. And there was no sense in Lydia saying that, they had separated three years before he and Tamara got together, what business had Lydia with Tamara, or with him for that matter? Nonetheless, as he lay on his back in the bare, sterile ward with its cold atmosphere of loneliness, Alexei recalled how, on the day before the order appointing him was due to come through, Lydia phoned him and commanded imperiously: "Alexei, I'll be waiting for you at half past one on Pushkin Square, in the little park, to the left of the monument."

When Alexei arrived, Lydia was already standing there in a cheap woolen jacket, looking like a college student, and—Alexei noticed—concealing her nervousness or inner tension by tapping her shoe on the pavement, as though she were trying to work herself into some previously determined rhythm. Without any preliminaries, as though they had seen each other only yesterday, she launched into conversation:

"I heard you're going to take Ivan's job."

"How would you know about that? The order hasn't been signed yet."

"Sonya phoned me."

"Am I to take this as some intrigue of Ivan's?"

"Ivan's your friend, you know that."

"And yours."

"What of it? We're not talking about Ivan. That job's not for you. It'll finish you."

"The bosses think otherwise, and they know me too."

"I'm the only one who knows you. You don't really even know yourself...Ivan's talented, he's made for that job."

"So I'm a mediocrity?"

"Your gifts are just different. I'm not saying you won't be able to work, but you'll have to puff yourself up to fit your armchair properly and you'll die if they take it away from you. Real leaders have to be born, and it's a great pity that someone has put it into your head that you can make a career as an administrator."

"We spoke about my career before our divorce."

"Do whatever you like, I've warned you."

"Are you going already?"

"I have to do some shopping."

"How's our daughter?"

"She's well."

"Lydia! Wait..."

That was how she left him. At first he used to recall this conversation frequently, then less often, and then, during his holidays, he had told Tamara about it. Her only comment was: "She's upset because the moment she left you or you left her, you started to move up." And now once again this conversation was there implacably before him, just as his memory had recorded it.

Alexei felt well. The pain had not returned. It even seemed as though there had been some kind of medical error, that he was well, and the over-cautious doctors had taken some slight indisposition, some neuralgia, for an infarction. He would get up now, and tomorrow he would go to the office, there was so much work left unfinished. And again Alexei noticed that he was hardly thinking of Tamara at all. Actually she was sure to cope, she wouldn't let him die. She had what it takes, the high-flown spiritual stuff could come later—she wasn't Lydia!—first she'd feed up his body, she was probably "taking measures" now. He might be bored with her sometimes, and sometimes she irritated him with her opinions, but she supported him in all his subconscious hope and schemes. Unlike Lydia, she wasn't always thrusting into his face that "truth" that he was already so sick of hearing at college: "Alexei you're an average person, with an average intellect and an average spirit and average courage. And you should live according to your capabilities. Do your duty honestly and be happy with that. But you keep trying to jump over your own head, and you make yourself unhappy, and your daughter, and me. I love you the way you are, Alexei..." And the way she left me, Alexei thought, when they made me head of department. When instead of going to Vologda to teach in the institute—the two offers had come at the same time—I took the job in the ministry. And to this day she was still teaching German at school, making do on her hundred and sixty roubles a month and not taking any translations to make up her income, or any alimony from him.

Tamara was different. In his moments of hesitation, she always said to him: "Why bother to wait until you gather wisdom and experience? Gagarin went into space at twenty-six!" Probably it was Tamara, in her love for him, who had forced him to scramble up the career ladder. She always looked up at him from below. And how calm and organized his life had become when they had got together and he had moved to her flat on Preobrazhensky Square.

Outside the door of the ward he could hear Anna's jubilant twittering and a quiet, insinuating male voice. It was dark now outside the window, but a ray of reddish sunshine came in at the crack under the door—the west must be at the corridor side of the building; these young lovers simply could not bear to part. They clearly found a lot of meaning in standing there touching each other's hands, in speaking and drinking in the natural tones of each other's voices.

That was how he had loved Lydia—all the time: in college, when they got married, when they lived in rented flats, when their daughter was born. Everything about Lydia was interesting, he loved everything about her—her opinions, her habits, the paradoxical harshness of her judgments, her unobtrusive and calm love. Then why—it was the first time this thought had risen into Alexei's consciousness, because previously he had seen their divorce as simply the result of the irritation accumulated over the years over a difference in characters emphasized by the passage of time—why had he allowed himself to be corroded by the rust of insatiable ambition? Lydia had been right, he had stopped loving her when she had tried to protect him from work that was beyond his strength. She had been fighting for his soul, and he had thought that she was pouring out on him her resentment at her own failure in life—"only a teacher." He had once flung that at her: "You're only a teacher..." And he had simply sold himself to Tamara...That was why after six months' life with her had become, not actually boring, but uninteresting. It turned out that all he valued in her was her appearance—he could go to any reception with her without giving it a second thought, and then...there were the slippers she put out in the hall at the very moment when he was turning his key in the door of the flat.

When he was still living with Lydia, their ministry had bought out a performance at the Bolshoi Theater. There was a big international trade conference on, and that had given them the excuse to book *Romeo and Juliet*. They had invited all the foreign guests, and set aside the upper tiers for their own people. Alexei had not supposed that he would get a ticket, but in the middle of the day Yuri Sergeyevich had suddenly sent for him and held out two tickets, saying. "For the box, for you and your wife. The guests' box will be next to yours."

At home Lydia had said: "I won't go. We saw *Romeo* not long ago, with the same cast. And you'd probably rather sit and read a book. If they need an experienced interpreter, just in case, ask them straight out, and then you go, knowing that you're working, but as for going just to parade yourself and your wife in front of the bosses—forget it."

Later, when Alexei was already sitting in Ivan's chair, he had been tormented by these obligatory visits to theaters, embassies and cocktail receptions and the like. Every time he was bothered by his own unnatural behavior, by the time that all this fuss cost him, by the fact that he was forgetting the language and he had no time to sit down with a book and read Goethe or Thomas Mann in the original for his own satisfaction. Tamara was indefatigable. She got to know all his bosses' wives, and always knew precisely who was the host at the private party or the reception, who she should go over and talk to, which dress should be complimented. She enjoyed herself so much at these receptions that Alexei was unable to refuse her this trifling pleasure. And gradually, day by day, the black weariness accumulated and settled like strontium in his bones. Tamara was in a hurry to see the world and get to know people, but where was he hurrying to? There was nothing for it, he had to put up with it and reap what he had sown.

The last thing Alexei had time to think about before he was seized by another attack of the former unbearable pain was: don't torment yourself, don't look for reasons, don't rake up the painful past, you have to pull through somehow and then he would change everything, organize his life differently, now was not the time to think, or you were done for...but the pain came anyway. As though afraid of interrupting this expiatory agony, Alexei cautiously reached out and pressed the button. The whispering stopped, Anna ran in, and after a glance at him, immediately said:

"It'll be all right in a moment, I'll give you an injection..."

Having left the hospital behind—the hospital walls with their firmly closed windows were reflected for the final time in the driving mirror above the steering wheel—Tamara pondered for a moment whether to go home, as she had intended, or...Her nerves were taut, and she knew the only thing that could calm her was speed, the kind of speed that fused the trees into a dense green ribbon, cut through here and there, as though by a knife, by the forest cuttings, the broad clearings of felled trees, the transmission lines receding into the depths of the forest. Oh, how badly she needed to be able to reason calmly and coolly at this moment, to see the possible developments clearly, unobscured by emotions, to be able in her despair to make an instant decision, to bring all her powers of reason and experience, all her contacts to bear on achieving one solitary goal—strengthening the thread from which Alexei's life—and her own well-being—hung. She would take a brief time-out. Just relax for a moment, catch her breath, and then go on. And Tamara decided on half an hour around the ring road. A plan was taking vague shape in her head: the first thing she had to do was to take advice and look for—not sympathy, no, who needed those well-worn phrases that everyone knew so well—real, concrete help from Kirill! It would soon be the rush hour, the center was packed with cars, she would get there quicker on the ring road. Now she had a definite goal. Tamara turned the car round once again, the brakes squealed and the car heeled over on the turn, and darted forward like a hunting dog catching the scent.

At the exit on to the ring road the glass traffic-police booth flashed by like a fairground tent, with the traffic patrol's yellow Mercedes moored beside it, and there it was, the concrete surface she needed—step on the accelerator, and let your gloomy thoughts stream past as the speed calmed you. Tamara's dark blue Zhiguli was now running in a herd of equally bright-colored cars.

Immediately she felt the usual relaxation, and at the edge of her consciousness there was the flicker of a thought which was cruel in its positive certainty: Whatever might happen, the Zhiguli will go on serving me and carrying me over the roads for a long time yet. It's a good thing we managed to buy a car already. There's no way I could get such a cheap and reliable model on my own. Tamara immediately felt guilty for such an inappropriate thought: she, probably really was a vile and calculating woman. And then she immediately furiously contradicted herself. Why was she calculating? Why did so many people think she was? She was simply persistent. She had got everything out of life by working hard for it. Yes, including the car. She'd bought it with her own money! Alexei had only got hold of it for her, or rather, the trade union committee had handed him on a plate the postcard which gave him the right to buy a car...

Tamara had first had the idea of buying a car at the age of fifteen. The war was not long over and her little Baltic town was chock-a-block with cars won as trophies in the action. After everything that she and her mother had been through, after the occupation and the famine, how wonderful and exciting life had suddenly become! Tamara was just graduating from secondary school, that is, she was still in the graduating class. Oh, the dresses that her mother used to make for her then, the virtuoso skill with which she reworked cast-offs! All the girls from their class were prime specimens, all tall and graceful, and how they all danced, whirling around the floor in the Officers' Club with the young golden-epauletted lieutenants! And during the third and the fourth year after Victory Day, all the girls found themselves a husband. But happiness seemed to be denied to Tamara. She danced better than anyone else in the class, and she was a good student, and she knew foreign languages—a rare thing at the time—she'd learned English from a self-study course, and she understood German, but she was just unlucky. Things just would not turn out right for her. But her mother used to say, "Darling, the main thing is not to make a mistake, to pick someone who is right for you..." And she spent two whole years dancing at the Officers' Club with all the lieutenants she knew. Then the experienced old woman who collected the tickets there said to her: "Tamara, you should buy a car, that lends a woman a certain special attraction..." In those days the captured BMWs were not so expensive, some mechanics she knew overhauled a car for her—and Tamara sat at the wheel for the first time in her life.

It was true, things began to improve. Picnics, visits to someone's dacha, midnight bathing—merry crowds, social bustle, flirting kisses, near-declarations. The captured car worked, and the next year Tamara married the middle-aged director of the local drama theater, which meant that she must be destined to be an actress. What dresses her mother had sewn her for her debut, what flounces and lace trimmings and drawn-thread work they had! They were dresses fit for a queen, but somehow the debut didn't come off, although her husband had had high hopes of his wife's charm and youth. True, they drank a glass or two of champagne, and gave "three cheers," and said a few words about the new talent, but the talent failed to materialize. Clearly she lacked that little something, that touch of wildness that would have given her talent the chance to blossom. And she so yearned for a brilliant life, surrounded by admiration, with something better to look forward to each day... But all the good things were past in a flash in her youth. Soon after her unsuccessful stage debut her husband went back to his old wife, the car broke down and she was sacked from the theater. Life seemed to have taken everything away from her. And then Tamara toughened up, and promised herself that she would get whatever she wanted. But she realized one thing, that she would have to go about it differently, her strategy was no longer frontal assault, but long-term siege. Life was less lively after that: in seven years she graduated from the correspondence course of the Library Institute, married a man who had moved there from Moscow, moved back to Moscow with him, got divorced, swapped his living-space allocation for two different ones, found herself a job where she was efficient and punctual, began to scrape together a little bit of money, bought a cooperative flat and some furniture, and when she looked around—she was thirty-seven, and she still hadn't got what she wanted. All her chances in life were used up, and if she hadn't happened to meet Alexei...

The familiar blue panels with the names of intersections, highways out of Moscow and towns flew past like cards being shuffled, and with every kilometer that hurtled by one clear and simple worldly-wise thought crystallized ever more clearly in Tamara's mind: she must not forget Alexei in his illness, but she also had a duty to herself. And how right she was never to put anything off till tomorrow. She had almost pulled it off, she had almost managed to live in West Germany. But people lived in Moscow too and were happy...

The car moved along at a good pace. She never had any doubts about the keenness of her eye, her nerve, her judgment and cool reactions. Forward, always forward, weaving in and out and scraping past the other cars, frightening the inexperienced private drivers, deftly shifting the gear lever, the clutch pedal and the brakes and impatiently encouraging the pedestrians with the illegal sound of the horn. To the right of the tall highway embankment there was a clear view of a region of new white blocks of Moscow flats, to the left there were cheerful little groves of trees with the first fuzzy green growth and the fanciful little fairground booths of the dachas, the movement might be swift and intense, but her soul could rest here, drinking in the green of the foliage, the tranquility of the early evening sky and the slack whistling of the wind. Gradually everything immediate, every care of the day was stripped away and everything began to seem not quite so bad, not quite so implacably determined. Her hopes now were all focused on Kirill. He never let her down at a difficult moment, although she knew exactly what he was. There was no point in pretending, when she had met Kirill, before Alexei, all her efforts to take him in hand had come to nothing. And Tamara was ten years younger than him and eight years younger than his wife. The two of them, Tamara and Kirill, were simply a match for each other...When one of Tamara's girl friends made an anonymous phone call to Kirill's wife and told her that he was seeing a young woman, the next day, as Kirill embraced Tamara, he had said: "Don't push too hard, my girl, it won't get you anywhere. Either everything stays the way it is, or you can find yourself someone else." Their parting had been easy, and they had remained friends; later she had even introduced him to Alexei.

Today Kirill would have to help, he was a doctor, he had a clinic, acquaintances, contacts...

Leaving the unlocked car at the gates of the clinic, she ran in at the entrance, went on up the stairs, without any white coat, and ran straight down the corridor past the patients, the orderlies, the nurses, the doctors with the stethoscopes on their chests. If only Kirill was there!

There was not a single visitor in the head doctor's cramped waiting room, the secretary was standing facing the window, brewing coffee on the electric ring on the window sill.

"Kirill," Tamara said as she burst into the surgery, "something's happened to Alexei!"

Kirill rose unhurriedly from his armchair and walked round his desk to Tamara.

"You have to help him."

"Don't worry, my dear. What's happened?"

"He's had a heart attack."

"I've had a heart attack too. As you can see, it's not fatal. He should have given up smoking a long time ago."

"He's forty years old, the worst possible age for a heart attack."

"Which hospital is he in?"

Tamara told him and added:

"You must phone them. I have to know the truth, no matter how bad it is."

"Natasha," said Kirill, bending over the intercom, "get me Sokolov on the phone."

"Vasili," Kirill said into the receiver, "how are you getting on?"

They spent a few minutes discussing some personal problems, inviting each other to come round, sending their best wishes to each other's wives, complaining about their medical personnel. Finally Kirill asked:

"You got a patient called Batashov in today. How bad is he?"

Kirill's face filled out, taking on a more serious expression.

"Not so good, you say. No, he's not a relative. Is there anything I can do to help?"

"Maybe there are some medicines he needs," Tamara interrupted.

"You have everything? Okay, keep me informed, I'll give you a call tomorrow."

The two of them, Tamara and Kirill, gazed fixedly into each other's eyes.

Kirill stood up again, and keeping his gaze fixed on Tamara, walked slowly towards her.

"Well, what did he say?" Tamara burst out.

"The situation is serious. Extensive infarction and embolism."

"Maybe we should transfer Alexei to your clinic?"

"He's in good hands, and now is not the right time."

"Tell me, Kirill, is there any medicine, even an imported one that's impossible to get hold of, that might..."

"There's no medicine that acts like the water of life, just sprinkle it on and the patient gets up." Kirill smiled cautiously, and went on gazing into Tamara's eyes as he stood in front of her. "Calm down, my little girl," he said tenderly, and cautiously placed his hand on her shoulder.

"Don't touch me!" Tamara shook off his hand. "I was asking you if there's any medicine that helps the recovery better than others."

"There is, but it's too soon to talk about that."

"You phone. It's the doctor's job not to let Alexei die and mine to get him back on his feet as quickly as possible."

"It's too soon to talk about it."

"Phone!"

Kirill dialed the number reluctantly, he made his request and promised something in exchange. Then, without raising his head, he wrote something on a sheet of paper and handed it to Tamara.

"It's all here. They're expecting you, so get a move on—there's only forty minutes left of the working day."

I'm saved, Alexei is saved, Tamara thought as she ran. Now she had a new goal. The most important thing for her was not to have to wait, not to languish in the reins of fate, but to yoke fate and keep moving on!

The blue Zhiguli hurtled back out into the whirlpool of Moscow. Tamara had always been proud of her skill as a driver, and how badly she needed it in this crazy chase!

The hardest thing was to hold herself back, but Tamara knew that was her only salvation. She only had to run through a red light, break the speed limit, violate any traffic rule, and if she was caught it would mean ten minutes explaining things to the traffic police. She clenched her teeth and held her old habits as an inveterate road bandit in check. She couldn't take any risks. Things she had got away with a dozen times before might mean disaster today. But nonetheless she didn't lose hope. After she'd spoken with Kirill everything didn't seem so dismal. She firmly believed that the doctors would do their job—not many people died from their first heart attack these days, and when it came down to it, it was the doctors' duty, they were responsible, that was what they were paid for...And she for her part wouldn't forget a single detail...As she waited at the red light at crossroads, she worked it out: for another day or two they wouldn't let anyone in to see Alexei, but she needn't worry, the doctors wouldn't take their eyes off him, and then later, when the crisis was past, she wouldn't trust the public nurses, she would sit at his bedside herself, and make them put an armchair or a bed into the ward for her—she knew that could be done—and for the time she was at work, she would have to find a nurse to sit at Alexei's bedside throughout those eight hours and anticipate his every wish. The routine had to be absolutely strict. Meals by the hour and the minute, massage, make Alexei do some light exercises, make sure the medicines were taken and all the procedures followed exactly on time. Everything had to be planned precisely, right down to when to open the window: none of that hospital food, with the tinned juice, everything had to be freshly prepared, with vegetables and fruit from the market. And then Tamara's memory, like an electronic calculator, clicked out something one of her girl friends had said a year ago about a wonderful nurse somewhere in Moscow, a retired actress, who got heart attack victims up on their feet in scarcely more than a month. That was it then, thought Tamara. First get the medicine, then go to Zhanna's to get the address of the old actress, then to the electrical goods shop for a juice extractor, find the old crone and then get home to the phone as quickly as possible. Then phone Nina, she was married to Perelman, the great lung specialist; of course, Kirill had phoned Sokolov, but if Perelman phoned too, the result would be better. Fly onwards, Zhiguli, only let the petrol last so there'll be no need to stop to fill the tank.

Tamara reached home at about ten.

When she went into the flat, she suddenly felt afraid. Everything was in its place. The furniture gleamed with polish, the cut crystal gleamed, the carpet on the floor glowed bright-red. But all this accumulated domestic luxury was suddenly obscured for Tamara by a nakedly simple thought: the curtain had already fallen, the actors had left the stage and the scenery no longer had any meaning. She had never used all these things for anything: the sideboard and the crystal, like the Zhiguli, had only served to emphasize and demonstrate for her, for her and Alexei, for their friends and acquaintances, the special nature and significance of Tamara's position. And if, God forbid, something serious should happen to Alexei, all this carefully constructed interior, too carefully constructed to be a home, which was good for entertaining guests, and holding dinners and suppers, but not for living in, because the only space left here for normal human life was the small bedroom, where Alexei's tiny desk, almost as small as a schoolboy's, huddled beside the wardrobe and the beds—if something serious should happen, then all this comfort would lose any meaning.

Before Alexei moved in with her, all this ostentatious wealth, all these refined reproductions and touching little nicknacks had screamed in proclamation of Tamara's exceptional subtlety of spirit and her tender heart, they were a subtle, not over-obvious bait: the first thing the refinement surrounding Tamara said to everyone was that the beautiful and tragic princess was waiting to be awoken by the prince's kiss. In Alexei's time, of course, more things had been added, the items had become more sumptuous, and the range wider, as everything had begun to serve another purpose: the highly-paid and tactful prince had arrived, and the things were called upon once again to cast their glow upon the chosen one: for their exceptional qualities of spirit the princess and the prince—a magnificently public couple—deserved the very best of fates and the most substantial endowment, everything that was most perfect in life must be cast at the feet of their happiness. This was the message shouted by the rare English "Ronson" cigarette lighter, and the near-antique Japanese coffee set on the inlaid table, carefully covered with a thin sheet of glass, and the other "unique" things...

And suddenly today, this moment, in the cold light of the Czechoslovakian chandelier, all these imported things seemed overlaid with a dull patina, and a layer of dust. In this instant of precise understanding, the things seemed to have lost their aesthetic essence. As though she were looking at an X-ray, Tamana could suddenly see the false trademark on the near-antique porcelain and the plastic sheet imitation of green wood covering the chipboard of the sideboards, she could see quite clearly the crude ribs of the framework of the wardrobes, the coarse cardboard showing beneath the reproductions, and the artistically arranged branches in the vases were no more than broken, withered twigs. The flat had lost its soul. She knew it had, because with Alexei's departure its mistress had lost her future. Forever. She would never rise again.

How could she have forgotten about Alexei at a time like this? How was he? Why all this fuss over these absurd and unnecessary matters? Just as long as he...

She dashed to the phone.

The duty orderly at the hospital said:

"Alexei Batashov died of cardiac arrest an hour ago."

Born in 1935, in Moscow, Sergei Yesin is a graduate of the Philology Department of Moscow University. He started writing in 1969 and is the author of widely popular collections of short stories and novels. He still lives in Moscow. This story was translated by Andrew Bromfield.

"When she regains consciousness, she tells her relatives that they are a bunch of idiots..."

The Inferno

BY FADIL HADZICH

IT'S eleven o'clock. The summer sun is scorching. I am walking into the post office of a little town on the Adriatic. A waiting room no larger than a train carriage is at the disposal of forty thousand tourists and ten thousand natives.

Right at this moment there are no more than six hundred people elbowing their way to the counter windows. Four hundred people are waiting for the phone, staring as if hypnotized at the three booths. The rest are sending off cables, having money wired to them or are trying to get out, with their tongues hanging out of their mouths, upon being told after three hours of waiting that nobody answered the phone in Tuzla or Frankfurt.

I have an insane idea to send off a cable today. I am making my way on all fours, creeping beneath an Italian, a German woman, and two citizens of our country, to the service window, and with a dexterous motion I grab a cable form. The Austrian (I recognize his accent) steps on my fingers and asks me what I'm looking for on the floor. With another hand he is clutching his wallet tightly, a clear allusion that he holds me for a pickpocket of tourists.

I don't give up. I pinch the Austrian's thigh, he shrieks and vanishes in the embrace of the German lady who stood next to him. Because of his indecent forwardness, she yells at the Austrian whose head is shaved. I withdraw two or three meters and fill in the cable form on the floor, marvelously protected by the round legs of a Swedish woman in jeans. It does not bother her since it's better that I am on the floor than leaning on her like the majority of those present in the waiting room.

The cable is a bit illegible. For the first time I am writing a cable in the position of a bird searching for a worm in the bark of a tree, with its head lowered. At the moment when I am filling in the name of sender, I am kicked sharply in my butt by a man who would certainly make it in soccer. Together with me, like in a bowling alley, five more people fall, piled atop each other like layers of a chocolate cake, except that instead of chocolate between us, there is stinking sweat characteristic of the tourists who have rented rooms without bathrooms.

I don't lose hope that I will manage to submit my cable. I am becoming religious, expecting that God will intercede for me. Suddenly two paramedics run in, stepping over our feet, and drag a man out of the booth who has learned that his apartment in Osijek has been broken into. That, of course, is not the fault of the post office but after six hours of waiting, to learn that you have been thoroughly burglarized acts like a flood after an earthquake of nine on the Richter scale. Two disasters don't go hand in hand, say the people who have never been to the small post offices of our Adriatic in August.

A well-fed citizen in shorts fans himself with a newspaper, shouting he'll die of a heart attack if they don't let him jump the line. A slim lady in her late twenties laughs in his face, unbuttons her blouse and asks him flirtatiously, if he doesn't think she is also suffering from the heat.

Everybody agrees that she is, and the fat man in shorts repeats for the last time that he will get a heart attack and, indeed, he collapses on the floor. Two citizens readily take nitroglycerin out of their pockets and revive him, and then let him jump the line, treating him like a dead man who's come back to life for a moment.

In front of the third telephone booth, there is a small war going on. Three men are wrestling, hitting everybody around them with elbows, and each one of them claims that his name was called over the loudspeakers to enter the booth. The voice of the phone operator is so soft and melodious that all names sound alike. Only when you take the receiver and hear the voice of a wrong aunt from a wrong town, you realize that the operator had called out the other guy, whom you left lying in front of the booth after almost plucking out his eyes.

That is all a minor thing compared to the man who has just received money and is very slowly counting it, until a nervous gentleman behind him snatches the money out of his hands and throws it up in the air—thinking that the man provokes the people who are kept waiting by his long and pedantic counting. Money which flies up in the air among so many people never reaches the floor and cannot be collected. The only option left is that the injured party fight for each dinar which he got by money order. The net result is a deficit of fifty thousand old dinars; not much, considering how much people overspend this time of the year.

A woman of dramatic appearance is elbowing her way into the first phone booth, after her name was called out over the speakers. She had received a cable this morning to call home in Ljubljana. Anxiously, she seizes the receiver and learns that nothing had happened; they only wanted to know how she is doing at the coast. Having wasted the whole morning worrying and waiting for the connection, the woman collapses; she had thought somebody had died in Ljubljana. When she regains consciousness, she tells her relatives that they are a bunch of idiots to send her a cable like that.

The post office is not responsible for this lady either.

In the other phone booth, both husband and wife shriek simultaneously, trying to say all they had planned to before the connection is broken off. The heat is unbearable, resulting in an atmosphere which is described very well in the work of Dante Alghieri in *Divine Comedy*.

Two hundred more people have arrived in the waiting room in the meantime. I have reached the window and on my horizon I make out the face of the woman who will take my cable. She is going about her business in the slow motion of a woman who is creating a design. Somebody shouts through his teeth that she should work a bit faster, but she does not. Instead, she leaves for the room at the end of the waiting room and mysteriously spends ten minutes there. "She is getting back at us," someone says from the queue. The one who is mumbling sticks to my back like a leech. I feel his heartbeat and try to decide whether the stench emanating from beneath his shirt is a cheap perfume or something even worse.

A clerk is touching up her hair and making up her lips. The closing time is nearing. I am trying to figure out whether I will make it to the counter; two people behind me resign from their strategic positions. One of them whispers in the tone of voice of a man who is capable of anything: "I'm going to kill someone today!" Then he swallows a pill, and hits the wall with his head, because it is not the door through which he'd hoped to pass.

The post office is not to blame for these scenes and in the apothecary of the small town, where forty thousand tourists buy aspirins and other pills, one can see even more stirring scenes. But there at least there is first aid medicine at hand.

Two minutes before closing time I hand in my cable, and

kiss the hand of the clerk (a woman) euphorically, in the manner of a genteel Pole. She asks me in the voice of a village teacher if I am not ill. I say I feel quite fine. She doesn't believe me and tells me to look at my reflection in the looking glass. She is right, I have black rings around my eyes and have aged several years. "You must rest more," says the motherly clerk, and in slow motion strikes my cable with a seal.

I turn to the door to attempt a breakthrough to the outside world. People refuse to leave though the post office is now officially closed. One of them explains to me his love for the post office:

"If I leave right now, in the afternoon I'll have to stand in line again, and this moment I'm in the splendid fifty-fourth place."

Then he lies down on the cement next to the German lady who has been waiting for her connection to Hamburg for three days; in a fever she is reciting Goethe, learned by heart at school.

This is Fadil Hadzich's second story to be published in English, the first, "Door Handle," appeared in SSI No. 83. A very pleasant person, Mr. Hadzich is a major Yugoslav writer, well known in Eastern Europe and the USSR. He has written several collections of short stories and a number of novels and screenplays. He has also written and produced a dozen plays. His translator, Josip Novakovich, immigrated to the USA fourteen years ago. Mr. Novakovich is himself a published short story writer.

For readers who can't read...

Greek, Arabic, Chinese, Japanese, Dutch, Norwegian, Chukchi, Finnish, Hindi, Turkish, Urdu, Hebrew, Russian, Vietnamese, Portuguese, etc., etc.

Short Story International takes you to all points of the compass, to anywhere in the world. There are intriguing stories waiting for you in future issues of SSI—stories that will involve you in corners of this world you've never seen...and in worlds outside this one...with glimpses into the future as well as the past, revealing fascinating, universal truths that bypass differences in language and point up similarities in people.

Send in the coupon below and every other month SSI will take you on a world cruise via the best short stories being published throughout the world today—the best entertainment gleaned from the work of the great creative writers who are enhancing the oldest expression of the entertainment arts—the short story.

A Harvest of the World's
Best Contemporary Writing Selected
and Published Every Other Month

Please enter my subscription to
Short Story International
P.O. Box 405, Great Neck, New York 11022
Six Issues for $24, U.S. & U.S. Possessions
Canada $27 (US), All Other Countries $29 (US)
Enclosed is my check for $ _____ for _____ subscriptions.

Name _____

Address _____

City _____ State _____ Zip _____

Country _____

Please check   ☐ *New Subscription*   ☐ *Renewal*

Gift for:

Name _____

Address _____

City _____State_____ Zip_____

Country _____

Please check ▢ New Subscription   ▢ Renewal

Gift for:

Name _____

Address _____

City _____State_____ Zip_____

Country _____

Please check ▢ New Subscription   ▢ Renewal

Gift for:

Name _____

Address _____

City _____State_____ Zip_____

Country _____

Please check ▢ New Subscription   ▢ Renewal

Gift for:

Name _____

Address _____

City _____State_____ Zip_____

Country _____

Please check ▢ New Subscription   ▢ Renewal

Gift for:

Name _____

Address _____

City _____State_____ Zip_____

Country _____

Please check ▢ New Subscription   ▢ Renewal

Gift for:

Name _____

Address _____

City _____State_____ Zip_____

Country _____

Please check ▢ New Subscription   ▢ Renewal

For the young people in your life...

The world of the short story for young people is inviting, exciting, rich in culture and tradition of near and far corners of the earth. *You* hold the key to this world...a world you can unlock for the young in your life...and inspire in them a genuine love for reading. We can think of few things which will give them as much lifelong pleasure as the habit of reading.

Seedling Series is directed to elementary readers (grades 4-7), and **Student Series** is geared to junior and senior high school readers.

Our stories from all lands are carefully selected to promote and strengthen the reading habit.

Give a Harvest of the World's Best Short Stories
Published Four Times a Year for Growing Minds.

Please enter my subscription(s) to:

_____ **Seedling Series: Short Story International**
$16 U.S. & U.S. Possessions
Canada $18 (U.S.) All Other Countries $19 (U.S.)

_____ Student Series: Short Story International
$18 U.S. & U.S. Possessions
Canada $20 (U.S.) All Other Countries $21 (U.S.)

Mail with check to:
Short Story International
P.O. Box 405, Great Neck, New York 11022

Donor: Name _____
Address _____
City _____ State _____ Zip _____
Country _____

Send To: Name _____
Address _____
City _____ State _____ Zip _____
Country _____
Please check ☐ *New Subscription*   ☐ *Renewal*

Send To: Name _____
Address _____
City _____ State _____ Zip _____
Country _____
Please check ☐ *New Subscription*   ☐ *Renewal*